THE
BLUE
LION

THE BLUE LION

An historical love story

GRAHAM BILLING

CAPE CATLEY LTD

ARTS COUNCIL OF NEW ZEALAND TOI AOTEAROA

This book has been written and published with the assistance of grants from Creative New Zealand

First published 2002
Cape Catley Ltd
Ngataringa Road
P O Box 32-622
Devonport, Auckland
New Zealand

Email: cape.catley@xtra.co.nz
Website: www.capecatleybooks.co.nz

© the estate of Graham Billing 2002

The author has asserted his moral right. The book is copyright under the Berne Conventiion. All rights reserved. No reproduction without permission. Inquiries should be made to the publishers.

Typeset in Weiss 11/14 pt.

Designed and typeset by Kate Greenaway, Auckland
Cover by Christine Cathie Design, Auckland
Printed by the Publishing Press, Auckland.

ISBN: 0-908561-92-X

AUTHOR'S NOTE

The idea for this book came from a reading of G.M. Thomson's *The Naturalisation of Animals and Plants in New Zealand* (Cambridge University Press, 1922), particularly text and footnotes concerning attempts to introduce Atlantic salmon to Otago.

Apart from passing reference to Sir James Hector and Sir Julius Vogel, the characters are fictitious and imagined. The character of Dan is imaginary but arose from a reading of the journal of Daniel Brock who accompanied Captain Charles Sturt on his expedition into the South Australian desert in 1843.

Spirogyra mud has been found in glaciated regions of the South Island of New Zealand but Epsomite has not been found in commercial quantities, and Logan Salpetreux's discovery of it is surmise. My Tarot divinations are derived from Aleister Crowley's *Book of Thoth*, Robert Wang's *Qabalistic Tarot* and readings published by Cartomancie Grimaud, of France.

Wellington,
New Zealand.
September 30, 2001

Graham Billing died, suddenly, at his home on December 12, 2001.

DEDICATION

To my parents and ancestors who bore me and to my children and their mother and their children and any human progeny who might thereafter be permitted to be conceived.

Also by Graham Billing:
Novels:
Forbush and the Penguins
The Alpha Trip
Statues
The Slipway
The Primal Therapy of Tom Purslane
The Chambered Nautilus
The Lifeboat

Poetry:
Changing Countries

Documentary:
New Zealand: The Sunlit Land
South: Man and Nature In Antarctica
The New Zealanders

ONE

Albion Duffy stood in the middle of Charlotte's kitchen, holding the ear of threshed wheat. He could feel, in its flailed slackness, the places where the plump grains had lain in their pale rows on each side of the stalk, falling from his fingers onto the scuffed wooden floor even now, as though he had weilded the flail. As though his shoulders ached from the work and his legs ached stiffly as he stood aside from the task, as if he were picking up the shovel to fling the grain high in the air so that the wind could winnow away the dust and chaff. He felt his body taut like the tendon in a bow. He seemed to rock his pelvis back, stretching on his toes, beautiful-bummed with the food grain, as if he were with woman.

    Her laugh broke in on him again as he watched her yanking with a crowbar at the nails of the wooden packing case which covered the parts, packed in wheaten straw, of her new iron stove. With each heave of the packing timber against the nails she laughed in company with the metal screech, her dark eyes grew wider and a strand or two more of her hair fell from her clean combed head across her forehead. He could see the red among the brown. She brushed away a fine strand of yellow straw from her top lip, where it had stuck, and looked at him.

"It will be a good stove, I know, and it will fit among the bricks just as I have had them made and the chimney will fit too, won't it?"

"It seems to me you've had a very good job done there," Albion said. He looked around the kitchen, at the broad red pine table with its tucked-in mahogany chairs with green plush bottoms, at the tall dresser with its rose and warratah plates, its willow pattern bowls and crystal water jugs, at the bench with its array of black iron pots and tin basins, at the gaping hole of an open trapdoor in the floor with its dim flight of wooden stairs going down into darkness. The stove bed of well-laid bricks seemed ready and level.

Charlotte Brosnahan wrenched away a whole side of the packing case, spilling straw and dust across the floor. The body of the stove was revealed. It looked to Albion as if it would not be too heavy to manhandle onto the prepared bricks. Together they heaved at the ends, clumsily lifted the iron and half slid it across the floor.

"One huge lift," said Charlotte, "and we'll have it in place," and when that was done, "I suppose that was right and we can put the doors and plates on next." She began to wrench at another packing case which contained the doors.

"What about the flue?" Albion said.

"I've had that made by the chimney man. It's all fitted in and ready. All it needs is the cap to stop the rain coming in when everything's in place." She wrenched again with the crowbar and the doors and plates fell out. There was lettering engraved and embossed on the doors.

"The light's too dim — I can't read what it says."

Albion stepped forward, searching in his pocket for a tin box of matches.

"You'll be able to read by the light." He struck a match on the roughened side of the box. As it flamed, a piece of burning phosphorus spun off into the straw. A gust of heat and flame immediately engulfed Charlotte. Albion dashed to a bucket of water standing by the bench. He flung it on the burning straw which was curling evilly in the orange flames. Charlotte's buttoned boots were soaked along with the hem of her skirt but the fire was out. He looked at her. Wisps of her hair were curled and brown. Her eyebrows were singed.

Together they leaned on the packing case, breathing hard. "That was a close-run thing," Charlotte said. "I'd lose everything if this place burned down — everything I've struggled for in this town full of struggles. Thank you for being so handy with the bucket."

"It burnt you. It nearly set fire to your blouse." Suddenly he imagined her without the blouse. "You're not wearing stays." He was immediately embarassed at this personal statement because they were strangers.

"Is my face bad? I don't need them." She laughed. "That's why men like me. I don't need stays."

Albion could now read the writing on the stove door. It simply gave the maker's name and place of manufacture.

"Are you all right? We only have to fit these things together now. You still look all right to me."

Together they fitted the stove doors on their hinges. They placed the lids on the fire box. They screwed the brass tap into the water reservoir with a thread of oakum to stop the drips. She handed him the flue cover.

"There's a ladder outside against the roof. Can you put this up for me?"

Outside the kitchen door Albion noticed the hen house, the vegetable garden, the small meadow stretching up McClaggan Street beside the flaxy stream, the cows, Jersey and Ayrshire, an empty pig sty, rose bushes, tall hollyhocks. He did not like heights and climbed the ladder carefully, then scrambled up the roof. It was of good Welsh slate, shipped out for the better buildings of the settlement. His boots did not slip on it, and grasping the chimney in both arms he put the top on the flue and looked about. This was the roof of Lancaster House, Charlotte's boarding house. In the high January sun he could see out over Dunedin. Smoke from the cooking fires and small factories was blowing away on the north-east wind that came down the harbour. The tallest buildings were churches with their spires among what seemed a disordered network of unpaved streets. Charlotte was standing at the bottom of the ladder when he came down.

"Now you could take the wood out and chop it up for the fire," she said. He did not like the way that she seemed to give orders. But then she said, "I'll sweep up the straw while you're doing it. I don't mind. The maids are busy upstairs." He had to agree that he would chop wood. There was a chopping block and axe in the yard and he had soon made a pile of kindling. He put it into the stove grate on top of the straw she had swept up.

"Is there coal?"

"Plenty of good coal," she said, pointing to a full bucket. "Henry Jubes brings it from Brighton on his bullock waggon."

Albion lit another match. He put coals on the blazing wood.

"Come and see the smoke," and she took his hand and drew him into the yard.

"I owe all this to James Lancaster," she said as they watched the chimney. "He made a fortune in the gold rush. He built this house and then decided to go into shipping. Everything comes here across the sea. He thought he could make a lot more money. So he gave this place to me." She seemed sad. "He told me that he owed me a lot. And he liked little Gregory."

"Gregory?"

"My son. He's at school this morning."

"You haven't filled the stove reservoir. We'd better do that now," he said.

They hoisted water to fill buckets in the yard, and in the kitchen he put more coal on the fire.

"What's down there?" he said, pointing towards the trapdoor.

"Come and see. Give me your matches." She lit an oil lamp from the bench. He followed her through the trapdoor and down the steep stairs. In the cellar he could hear water trickling.

"James had to put in a pipe to take water from the creek. It keeps this place cool." On the walls he could dimly see shelving. Glass jars of fruit and vegetable sealed with wax lined the shelves. She stood with her face half lit by the lamp and half by the light of the trapdoor. She was very close and he could see the burnt wisps of her hair and eyebrows. With an unsteady hand he wiped away the golden frizzled strands and rubbed them from his fingers. She said nothing but looked up at him as if he were quite familiar to her. She leaned towards him briefly.

"I would be happy to have you as a lodger," she said when they had ascended to the kitchen. She made him go first so that he would not see into her skirts. "How long will you stay?"

"I don't know. Is that all right?"

"Perfectly," she said as he excused himself and went out the door. "You'll find it," she called. "We don't have proper sewers yet. People leave their . . . um . . . I mustn't say it . . . ex . . . waste in the flax bushes along the creek."

He went off to the outhouse with its tin bucket, feeling proud of her for finding the right word. Inside, the corrugated iron walls were painted a tarry black that had crazed. The outside had been white with a blue roof, like a pavilion, he had thought as he went in. Now he wondered, as he sat on the smooth wood, what he was going to do with his new life. In the iron heat he shifted as he remembered. He had liked Charlotte and was pleased that Dan Cockle had brought him here. She had appealed to him as a woman and he had not been with a woman since he was with a whore at a dockside bar in Wellington. That one had come on him while he was peeing in the stone toilet and boldy asked, "Can I hold it for you?" With many misgivings he had let her and before long found himself taking a room for the night but had to satisfy himself without entering her because he was afraid of disease. He had liked her darkness and the low cut of her dress like Fleet Street. Now the question of what he would do with his new life repeated itself. He had plenty of money left over from the sale of his parents' holding in Teesdale. He kept notes with him and had had a draft sent to the Bank of New Zealand.

Going to Dunedin had been spontaneous. There was a schooner sailing down the coast from Wellington. In her tiny midships cabin he had stowed his canvas kit with his clothes, his bag of oatmeal and tin of molasses and small bottle of salt, and a leather bag of earth that he kept damp so that the tarragon root would stay alive, and his pack of Tarot cards. Days later, after beating into a strong southerly in cold discomfort, he had come on deck to find the boat more kindly in the sea, the sun shining with a following north-east wind and the comfortable dark green of the Otago coast amidships to starboard as they ran. The schooner's wooden deck was silvery with sea water. It ran about as they rolled and wet the toes of the dark leather riding boots he had bought in Australia. Spray still seemed to glisten on the rigging, the topsail yard and the huge grey mainsail that curved above him.

Inside the harbour heads they had run down the bright channel, pushing now and then through drifts of rubbish and night soil that were dropped in the tide every few days from barges filled in Dunedin. Then they were past painted Port Chalmers, Goat Island and Quarantine Island and on to the town smoke that was lifted up and blown beyond Saddle Hill in the south. He could recognise such landmarks from pictures he had seen in Wellington. The schooner downed sails with the wooden luff rings rattling on the masts and nudged alongside a raft of small coasters tied up at a wharf in the Basin.

Albion was not sorry to leave the mournful sailors. Having lived close to them for several days he had decided that watching what they did as they went about their duties at sail work or the wheel was more important than any speculation about what they thought. They obeyed orders. He would make that a rule of his life in the new country. He had looked into the sailors' eyes but had not seen any light. There was nothing stirring to the glance. They wore drab colours. He thought now that he was seeing things a man's way. That was the way he was.

Men were already jumping from the schooner upon other vessels, across their decks and up the ladder onto the wharf. With his kit on his shoulder he followed them, across decks and coiled ropes, fearful that he would slip. Down the wharf past the Customs Office there was one cab standing on Birch Street. The black horse was deep in a nose bag.

"I can take you anywhere you want to go," called a small man with a black beard standing there. "One and six for the first mile and a shilling a mile after that. Did you have a good trip?"

"I don't know the town," Albion said. His legs still felt wobbly after the schooner. "I need to find somewhere to stay."

"Right as rain," said the man. "I'm Dan Cockle. I used to be a bullocky in South Australia but now I like it here."

"Is it a good town?"

"Apart from the reverends." He paused and took the nosebag from the horse's neck. "But we changed all that. There's money here now. Because of the gold in the hills. There's been lots of Englishmen and Australians and Americans and a few Continentals too. I'll show you the town first."

The cab was open with its canvas back down. Dan sprang into his high seat and looked round and down at Albion.

"I'll take you to Lancaster House in McLaggan Street. Old James Lancaster made a lot of money in the Rush and then gave his house to Charlotte Brosnahan. She runs it for board now. You'll be right there."

It seemed to Albion that Dan had brought him to a good place but suddenly there was a beating on the tin roof which hurt his ears. Outside he saw that it was a monkey, a little brown monkey sitting on the roof, banging with a stick. It stopped banging and looked at him with round eyes, dark and shining. He wanted to reach out and stroke it but the roof was too high. It chattered at him softly, showing long canine teeth. Then it dropped the stick, jumped down into the grass and ran to the washing line. It sprang up to the line and swung along it until it reached the post, then sat on top of the post and seemed to grin at him.

"Don't worry about Tiny," called Charlotte from the kitchen door. "He's just an Anjer monkey Gregory's father gave me from the ship he was on. They live in the rigging of those Eastern ships. He's quite tame."

Albion looked about the garden. Beyond the washing line was a railed fence. In the sloping paddock that fell to the creek were two cows, a Jersey and a red and white Ayrshire, both horned. In a corner of the paddock was a low milking shed. The hen house was closer to him with its dozen Black Orpingtons and beside that the vegetable garden with cabbage and beet and lettuces, carrot and parsnip tops, a big potato bed with the dark green plants in flower. There were peas staked up, and turned bare earth where he supposed broad beans had been. A pile of split logs lay by the wood box and a red coal box with a sloping roof. There were apple trees, and pears and plums, small yet but heavy with fruit. There were gooseberry and currant bushes beside the house and a patch with thyme and sage and parsley. There would be room there, he thought, for some of the herb seeds he had brought, in packets, in his kit. The monkey jumped from the pole and ran across the grass to Charlotte. It jumped onto her shoulders and began to run its fingers over her hair, showing the dark prints of its palms.

"You'll be wanting something to eat," she said. "I've got some pork pies the grocer sent up. And after that I'll show you your room."

"Are these from your own pigs?" he asked as they sat at the kitchen table.

"I don't keep pigs," she said. "There's too much smell and killing — leave all that to the butcher. He's very good, I think." She pushed a bread board with a loaf on it to him and a plate with a round pat of fresh butter. "Have some of my jam. I made it last year from berries the Maoris call poroporo — we call it bully bull. I think it's related to the potato. They're big berries like olives."

"What about flour here?"

"The wheat comes from Silverstream, from the settlements on the Taieri Plain, over the south of Flagstaff Hill you can see up there. The bakers say it's a bit soft but it'll do."

"And the coal?"

"That comes from Brighton — on the sea side of Saddle Hill,

before you get to the mouth of the Taieri River. I had a friend called Logan Salpetreux. He reckoned there was lots of chemicals round here."

How capable she is, Albion thought as he lay on his bed, trying it out, later. The quilt was bright with browns and greens. Under it were soft blankets and a mattress that fitted his body.

"Take your boots off," he heard his mother say, admonishing him.

"Oh leave me alone. The yard is not wet."

He could unpack his kit, put his clothes in the little oak dresser, look in the mirror hanging in its oval wooden frame. His waistcoat felt too tight and he took out from its pocket the silver half-Hunter watch his father had left him. His curving long fingers snipped open the back of it and he watched the action of the wheels, feeling reassured. He closed it and opened the face. He pressed the knob and heard the watch strike two. All was well, then. He unbuttoned his waistcoat and felt his chin in the shaved part below his sideburns. She had told him that there were only a few lodgers in the house, that Dan Cockle had a room below him on the ground floor and would drive his cab into the bush with his gun and shoot birds for her table. Sometimes he would take his gun and catch the litle steam ferry to Anderson's Bay across the head of the harbour. He would shoot ducks on the inlets. There was a timber mill in the Leith Valley, in the stream running from the north-west of the town where water powered the saws, and stands of red pine were being cut up. He closed his eyes and could hear the scrubbing of the maid distantly. He would have dinner cooked on the new stove and meet the people who lived there. What would he *do*?

Downstairs in the kitchen again the little boy Gregory was now creeping around. He was about seven, Albion thought, born in 1860. He was very thin, blonde and pale with a snake-shaped diamond face, large eyes, almost a homunculus. Albion said hullo but Gregory just looked at him widely.

"Go and grind some shell grit for the hens," Charlotte said.

"Are there plenty of shells? Can I share the wheat out for them?" He spoke with a lisp.

"The kettle's boiling. Would you like tea now?" Charlotte asked and Albion did not know if she were talking to him or the boy but he stood at the kitchen door with his cup and watched the boy run to the hen house. Clouds had come over and rain began to fall. He watched Gregory crawl under some huge rhubarb leaves at the edge of the garden and take shelter. He curled up and could hardly be seen there. The monkey leapt down from the clothes line and bounded to curl up with him. He held the monkey as the rain became heavier and drops spun on the clay dust of the yard.

Charlotte stood beside Albion. She smelt of rose water. "Gregory loves it under the rhubarb when it rains. And with the monkey. Sometimes you can't tell they're there. At half past four I will give him his dinner. He will only eat eggs in pancakes made of oat meal, I'm afraid, but it means he will be in bed by the time we have supper. He's like his father — very determined, I thought." She paused. "He loves those hens. He gathers sorrel and chickweed and baby thistle leaves to feed them with."

"Do you have all those weeds here already?"

"Oh they come in the grass seed and the wheat. It's good, I think, isn't it?"

"Soon the garden will be full of English birds, too."

"They bring them in the ships and let them go all the time. There's even gorse and broom growing up the creek. It's like home."

"Where did you come from, then?"

"I came out as a girl. Only seventeen. I worked at the washing for a big house but then the ship came in that had Gregory's father. He was the bosun and they came from Bangkok with rice and tapioca and brass and teak and mahogany wood for furniture. I was English but Irish by breeding."

The cows were standing by the fence. A maid came by them, carrying a wooden pail. "Oh, this is Mavis. Say hullo to Mr Duffy. He's come to live. And put a shawl over you to keep the wet off."

"Tomorrow Dan will show me the town in his cab," Albion said. "It looked fair from the roof."

She looked up at him. "And where did you come from?"

"We had a farm in Yorkshire near Barnard Castle just below Teesdale. I helped work the farm till my father and mother died. I worked as a ghillie too. I took the gents fishing for salmon up the river and showed them the spots. I went away up in the moors and saw the salmon. They laid their eggs there."

"What will you do here?"

"I don't know yet. There ought to be work." Albion suddenly felt trapped. "Did you marry him?"

"Who?"

"The bosun. Gregory's father."

"Oh no. He sailed away. He promised but I've never seen him again. The stove needs more coal, I think."

He could hear the iron wheels of a dray in the rough street, the crack of a whip and the slow crunching of pulling bullocks.

"That must be Henry Jubes." She listened. "He usually comes past about now and has a cup of tea. Then he goes off with the team around the town and comes back for his supper." Faintly Albion could hear his watch strike three. The rain had stopped but there was now a breeze from the south. He felt colder and was glad of his heavy pale moleskin trousers and his dark tweed jacket.

"Time to start putting the dinner on. I'll wait for Mavis to finish the milking and then she can peel the vegetables. There's mutton tonight and I'll roast it slow in my new oven."

"I'll go up to my room. I haven't unpacked yet." Sun was out again and pale bands of light came through his Chinese slatted blind. He emptied his kit onto the bed, tipping it up, rummaging in the clothes and pulling them all out. He would put his treasures in the drawer under the mirror. He turned them over in his hands. There was a curved pruning saw which would have to go under the bed, and a long, broad knife in a leather sheath that would have to go under there, too. There was a brass locket on a chain with a painting of his mother inside it that could go in the drawer. There was his pack of Tarot cards, a bottle of black ink, some pen holders and steel nibs, a small book for addresses. Then there was a letter case which unlocked and had a blotter on the inside with some thick paper and envelopes in pockets. It would have to go in the oak dresser, in the top.

Wrapped in a fine white handkerchief there was his father's signet ring and his mother's wedding ring and gold engagement ring set with small rubies. There was his purse with coins and notes. There was his shaving brush and razor and a cake of yellow soap, his toothbrush and a bottle of iodine, his salt and oatmeal and molasses, and he put all these things away carefully. There was ointment for his toes but it did not seem to work. Probably he needed something with zinc in it. There were tin boxes of matches. He liked to collect matches, feeling that he never knew when he would need them. He put all these things away carefully.

He had two or three books, a copy of a Walter Scott novel, some of Carlyle's essays and some commentaries on Darwin. "Where's your Bible?" he heard his mother say but he did not have one. "I'm not keen on that any more, Mother." He had read Charles Lyell on the formation and age of the earth, too, and he remembered some works on physics and electricity.

"There's a lot to see, Mother," he said aloud. A bellbird was singing in the elderberry bush that had grown up by the hen house. He had heard bellbirds in Wellington.

Embarrassed at being asked so soon to carve the meat, Albion sat down at the kitchen table and took the bone-handled carving knife and fork to a leg of roast mutton. On the table Dolly the housemaid, peremptory, he thought, with her frizzled blonde hair under her white cap and her thin waist, had put out dishes of potatoes, leeks and peas. With a heavy spoon there was a large boat of white sauce rich with chopped capers which steamed beside him.

"The grocer's just got in a new barrel," Charlotte said to the table. Sitting there, still in their work clothes, were Thora Hardcastle, Henry, Dan, a pale girl called Yvonne and John Wilkes.

"Thora manages the shop where her women do sewing," Charlotte said, "and this is Yvonne who works for her, and Henry who came in from his dray — the bullocks get un-yoked in the stable yards down the street and go to their hay — and Mr Wilkes who is in charge of the cutting on the hill they're making along Princes Street to the Octagon. There's a lot of talk because of the steps being put in behind the brewery."

John Wilkes began to laugh, leaning forward and looking intently at Albion's carving. "A good bit of meat, Mrs Brosnahan. There's a lot of talk about those steps. They say the women shouldn't use them. They're so steep and the men could see the petticoats."

So they called her Mrs Brosnahan, because of her son, he supposed. Thora Hardcastle was a stern woman, straight in a dark dress with big sleeves. He could see that Yvonne's fingers were red from her sewing. "Not too much for me," Thora said, her mouth in a firm line under her beaked nose and the wire glasses over her eyes like vegetables.

"Of all the people I drive," said Dan, "they all seem to want the old horse to hurry and I haven't time for that. They have to take what comes."

"Aye," Henry said. "You should go back to bullocking maybe. You just have to crack the whip over them quietly and call their names and they'll push on for you. It never did anybody any good to rush." Dolly, waiting beside the table grudgingly, began to push the vegetable dishes around to them. Albion helped himself to large spoonfuls of caper sauce over his meat. Thora's stomach rumbled.

"There's a rice pudding with custard from the hens' eggs and we've stewed some of the plums," Charlotte said but nobody replied. Dolly went round with a glass jug and poured water in all of their tumblers. Some spilled on the heavy linen tablecloth and even on Thora's silver napkin ring. "Clumsy girl,' she said, wiping it as if she was still in her work shop. Henry looked at her, amused, and the greying whiskers on his round face stood out.

"Come into the parlour, then," Charlotte said at last, "and Dolly will pour the tea, won't you Dolly."

In there it was so different from the yard with its well and its mossy brick surround under the rope and bucket hanging from a gibbet. The gold plush curtains were still drawn back and he could see across the creek valley to where the bush began, and the edge of the kitchen garden where Dolly had spread the vegetable peelings to be dug in. There were paintings on the walls, ladies in flowery hats, sailing ships full under mountains, towering over the shining chairs with their turned wooden backs and cane seats, a maple-wood piano in one corner, and a large couch covered with black leather and a tea table where Dolly now stood with ranked cups and a china pot with red leaves painted on it. Most of all, on a pedestal between the windows, was a lion, he thought, in bright blue glazed pottery, sitting on its haunches

"It's a dog, really," Charlotte said, seeing him looking. "Everybody thinks it a lion but it's a dog sitting. Grigori brought it from Burma — Gregory's father, you know. Grigori Basle, he was. He was Czech or Hungarian. He didn't quite know but his family settled in Basle in 1848 because of the peace of it and called themselves that. And he went down the Rhine for a sea-going life. That dog's grinning so. It's only a little Pekingese, a lap dog, a temple dog I think, but it grins away and looks like a little blue lion. That's how I always think of it, anyway. After Grigori."

"A blue lion from a temple," Albion said. "You wouldn't have thought to see it here."

"It takes all sorts, doesn't it." Thora sounded a little acid, holding her tea cup and seeming to sit uncomfortable on the edge of her chair.

"I always liked blue," Yvonne said from the sofa. It was the first time she had spoken, even over the meal in the kitchen. "It's a sort of greeny blue, isn't it. Like ducks have or rather peacocks, I think."

"That statue's president of the parlour," said Dan.

"Aye, and it's a dog grinning with its little ears pricked back and looking like a lion," Henry put in.

"Maybe you should get a real dog, Mrs Brosnahan," said John.

"I don't think so," said Charlotte. "Where would I find the time? But I've got a surprise for you all, anyway."

Everybody clinked their tea cups on their saucers. Dolly went out, looking very thin. Albion thought of the Lurcher dogs that used to be on the farm at home and how they would catch hares after the shoot and the hares would hang upside down in the stable while the blood dripped out of their noses into a bowl.

"You all know about the water, how there's a water company now as well as the gas works and they've piped the water down the main street and how they've decided to dig a sewer and line it with bricks so the water goes into the harbour and the tide. Well, I'm getting a bath."

Everybody began to talk at once, asking when they could use it.

"I suppose the bath will be connected to the sewer through some big clay pipes?" John said.

"Yes. And it'll have a plug you can pull out to drain the water away when you've finished. Everyone will have to have their bath night so the water can be heated in my new stove. A round plug made of layers of thick leather, I think. That's what I ordered and it's come on the schooner that brought Mr Duffy, I think."

"I'll cart it up in the morning before I start taking the muck from the cutting," Henry said. "It won't take long from the jetty."

"A bath, a long bath." Dan laughed. "No more washing in a little basin. A good long soak."

Bodies, Albion thought. Bones laid out, the Death card in the Tarot pack that meant renewal even though it was a skeleton with a scythe. Lying out in the heat.

"And I'll get lots of mutton fat from the butcher and I'll make lots of yellow soap with the wood ash for lye and dry it in my oven in."

Even Thora said, "And we will all be clean." It sounded like a prayer.

"I'll give you a tune on that," Dan said, opening the piano. Charlotte sang *The Last Rose of Summer* in a rich contralto voice.

TWO

He woke up with the sound of *Annie Laurie* still in his ears, mingled with the song of the bellbirds in the elderberry bush. Strong bars of light from the rising sun came through his Chinese blind.

"We'll not be needing that for a while,' he said, looking at the empty fireplace and putting his bare feet on the cool wooden floor instead of the rag rug with its pink and black square tufts. He slopped water from the ewer into the basin on the washstand and bathed his eyes coldly.

Dan was backing the black horse into the shafts of the cab in the stable. He liked the blue curtains on the windows of the maid's room above it, up the stairs. A dusty Surrey cart with a canvas hood was in there too, and a brougham with a broken driver's seat

"I just put a handful of oats in the bucket and rattle them and he comes across the paddock," Dan said as he raised the shafts to slide into the harness leather. "I put him out there at night when there's no dew. He likes to have a roll after I've rubbed him down of an evening. I reckon he was a trooper's horse before I bought him off the boat from Victoria. I broke him to the shafts and he doesn't shy at the smell of blood or the sight of a gun."

Albion hadn't seen the stable and its cobbled yard, its wide gate, behind the house. There were no chimneys for fires to keep the maids warm. He shut the stable doors after Dan walked the horse and cab out. A little smoke lay in the hollow at the bottom of the street. "Plenty of firewood for the bakers and blacksmiths," Dan called down to him in the back seat as they ambled towards the harbour. "First I have to call at the butchers for Charlotte." He swept his whip wide. "When the Rush was on, just five years ago now, all this was covered with shacks and tents. There were thousands coming from Australia and California, all the time for months." Behind the shop were pens for sheep and cattle and pigs. The butcher killed his own. Stone guttering ran with blood towards the water. The offal cart, already half full of heads and intestines, stood in the yard, dripping. "All this stuff gets dumped on the foreshore, along with the fire ashes. There's talk of a sewer line all the way out to the ocean but just now things go on the sand. But the tide doesn't wash it away — and for those that can afford the nightman to come, the stuff gets put in the barges and taken down towards the Heads. But the tide washes it back and the people at Port Chalmers keep complaining."

Dan put the meaty ribs of a bull calf under the seat. "I'll chop it up for her later." At the other end of town, up shingley Princess Street and George Street, stone broken with the hammer, he turned into Woodhaugh. "We'll go up the Bullock Track."

He slung the nosebag over the horse's neck. The track sidled up the side of a cliff. "They keep the drays at the top because it's so steep and they have to walk the bullocks up from here in single file to do the work on the hill." Trees with pale berries hung over the track. Dan took his gun as they climbed up. Parson birds flew away and Albion heard the soughing wings of wood pigeons. At the top, on the Clear they walked to the edge and looked down over the town, at Lake Logan, where the sea came in and a jetty ran out in the shallows, at the winding Leith and the first clearing of the Botanical Gardens with new wooden buildings going up. There were church spires on the flat and the brick hospital beginning to the south. "They've got gardeners there to grow flowers and make the town beautiful. That's all new - since I came here."

"When was that?"

"Two years ago now. Charlotte's house was already built."

"What about before that?"

"Stock inspector for the Government in Adelaide. Then I took a job with Captain Sturt who was going on his great expedition into the desert to look for a great lake there. I was the bird skinner. I had to shoot the birds and draw and paint them for him. The birds there, all kinds of colours, the cockatoos and parrots and ducks and swans and pelicans with their great dishy beaks, and the black fellahs all ashy hiding round the billabongs and catching fish. It was all right when it rained though it got cold then but mostly it was terrible heat and we had to sleep on the ground, wrapped up under the waggons with the bullocks turned out all bloody from the yokes, and thin. We got short of feed and coming back we got ill and the captain came rushing past us riding in his cart and wouldn't even spare us a bottle of vinegar for our skin and sickness. I'd had enough of him then. I was proud to leave.

"But this — this is all new and it gets cold but I make a living and I'm well fed. All that seems like a dream — more than twenty-five years ago. Then I went to Victoria and drove horses and a

California man brought out the Concord, a new coach from America, and started the coach line in Dunedin here and I heard about it and so I came. What about you?"

"My family had a farm — just a small place. Yeoman farmers you'd call them in the old way. But they died and I sold up and thought I'd try out here. I could pay for a cabin on a ship then. But it was a long slow haul to Sydney. And then I came over. I've got some in the bank but mostly just what I stand up in."

"You should have been married, then."

"I have to find the right woman, I suppose. It takes a lot of time."

"We'll go down now."

"What did you think of it?" they asked at supper. Albion put his knife and fork on the plate beside the leg bones of a pigeon that Dan had shot, remembering how it had sat fat and stupid in a dark tree with the sun gleaming on its white breast and its small blue-green head with its black orange-rimmed eyes nodding back and forth. "We went right up to Ross Creek where they've built the reservoir and Dan shot the birds up there, before we got to the big dam and climbed up to a forest of big bare trees."

"Old man manuka."

"And then we came back through the town and the stone buildings, over bridges made of logs but where they're putting up stone instead. All by the eye, Dan said. That's how they build them. Not even any plans. It's such a busy place. There's people everywhere and I even heard a factory whistle. I don't know where it was from but they must have a steam engine there to make the whistle. That must have been at noon and women came out into the streets. I was amazed."

Then, in the declining afternoon, he had wanted to smell a byre again and the smell of milk. He had walked across the yard, past a young pear tree that would soon be drunken with fruit, and a pruned apple, then under the rough rail of the fence and across to the shed where the Ayrshire waited and the Jersey stood with its neck in the bale, munching hay, while Mavis drew her milk down to a wooden bucket with a rope handle. He remembered the sight well, the maid on her stool, red hands on the teats, capped head pressed into the cow's yellow belly.

"Do you like to watch?" she said, in her black dress with the red flowers embroidered on it, red over an old silky material as if it had once been fine velvet. She laughed and looked sideways up at him, brown eyed, aging and thin over the white collar and narrow chest. "Try this!" She bent the nearest teat up and squirted a stream of milk at him. His thigh was wet. He brushed the milk down with his hand and a soaking stain grew. She laughed again. "Got you where you least wanted it, didn't I. Never mind — I've seen plenty of that in my time."

"Don't you want it any more?" Albion said. It was not appropriate, he knew immediately, but he had spoken by impulse.

"Too old for it, aren't I,' she said in a voice that he found very sad and bent her head towards the cow again.

Albion patted the cow's rump and walked off, feeling the damp on his leg. Once, when he was about three, he remembered, he had gone into his father's byre and the maid had squirted milk right into his mouth which was open in wonder at the milking. The milk ran down his chin. He could feel it and remember the grassy taste. The apples on the tree were beginning to colour, red bruises on the shining green.

"Henry's gone today for a load of coal from Brighton," Charlotte told the table. "And the bath arrived. I had it set up in the room in there and we can all look at it after the pudding."

"I never had a bath," Yvonne said softly.

"It's just what girls like you need," said Thora. "We all know everybody's got to be clean." Albion thought in a flash of the cow byre and the milk maid and felt his trousers to see if the stain was still there.

They stood at the door of the little room off the kitchen. "The drayman brought it. We had to be very careful not to chip the paint." The bath was long and low, of tin painted white with cross-pieces on the bottom to keep it steady. "There's not many baths here," she said. "They've got a special clause in the regulations for the Water Company that's doing the piping from Ross Creek. There's a special fee if you have a bath but I don't see that I'll have to pay it because they haven't put the water up here yet. The water will run into the creek down below and then into the sewer."

"It'll take quite a lot of hot water, won't it," Thora said.

"And nobody can christen it tonight because Dolly forgot to fill up the reservoir on the stove."

The bath was there, looking clean and grand, and a small table had been set up with a ewer and basin and a mirror over it. "The gentlemen can shave here rather than have the maid bringing the hot water to their rooms," Charlotte said. "They'll be able to get their own from the kettle on the stove. It's always hot. We had trouble screwing the drain pipe in. The drayman had to go away and get a short piece to fit onto the pipe into the creek and then cut a thread going the other way on it. But the plug fits nicely. I tried it."

Once again, as they moved into the parlour for tea, Albion thought how capable Charlotte was. Perhaps it had been all her experience doing the washing for a big house.

"I'll get a big bath one day," Charlotte said as they gathered around the tea table. "I'd like to have a big marble bath, all in pale pink and standing on a stone slab and the bath'll have claw feet. And somehow there'd be hot water coming down pipes to fill it up whenever you wanted just while you laid back and had your dreams."

There was silence for a long time.

"Cards," Dan said. "We all ought to play cards in here. We've got plenty of people here."

"I don't think we've got any cards — unless Mr Lancaster left some."

"Never mind. I'll buy some. But we better wait for Henry coming back. He's pretty good at cards."

"Do you play cards, Albion?" Charlotte looked at him with her round eyes. "You look like a bit of a gambler." She seemed to be teasing him.

I'm nothing of a gambler. Not at all."

"But you do play cards." She was insistent and he felt embarrassed. He began to blush, he thought.

"Only my own sort. They're just my own affair."

"Fortune cards, I bet. I bet you learned them from the gypsies or some such. You've got that look."

"Not fortune really? Can you tell the future? I don't really think you can."

"But you try, don't you. I can see you try. I bet you've got a pack of cards. Go and get your cards."

"Now, Charlotte — don't go getting into deep water," Dan said. "Well I'm off to have a rest."

When he had gone, and Thora and Yvonne too, Charlotte said, "Will you tell me my cards? Just for me? You don't have to give up any secrets. We'll be alone now."

Albion felt that his feet were tingling in his boots. "I suppose I could just do a very simple thing. But you have to realise that I wouldn't be saying anything about you, I think. I think I'd just be saying things about myself, about the way I see life, not anybody else. Well, yes, I"ve got a Tarot pack and I can do a very simple thing for you. I'll have to go and get them."

"We can put them out here." She sat down beside a small wooden table with an ivory inlay of elephants. "Grigori gave me this. It seems to go with the lion, or dog, whatever you think it is."

"I'll just do a simple cross," he said when he sat opposite her with the slippery cards. They were alone now. For some reason it seemed to be right that he was doing this with her whose hair was quite coppery in the lamp light. Tarot was just a game, he told himself, but it was an adventure into another person, or perhaps it was. At any rate he would see how she looked at the cards and would try to guess what she was thinking about them, to find out how she worked, he supposed. He could not help hoping that they would not find some great impediment, some great emanation of the past that still rose over her and made it seem as if he could never know her.

Quickly he dealt out the pack, face up and putting the twenty-two trump cards aside. When he had them he held them high in his right hand and shuffled them into his left. This would remove any evil forces that clung to the cards. Then he cut the pile from right to left three times. He noticed that she was trying to look amused and cynical, as if she was not prepared to believe anything that he told her the cards described. The gold drapes softly billowed into the room.

"The wind's changed," he said. "It must be round to the north again."

"It's never much at this time of night. You can smell the wood smoke on it, can't you." Her voice was quite soft. She watched the cards as he laid them out, face down, four in a cross.

"That's the present," he said, pointing to the card on her left, "and that's the future," the card on her right. At top and bottom he pointed to Thought and Fulfillment. "Don't hold your breath.

It's really very simple. You've just got to look at the cards and let yourself see what you see in them — let your mind go. And then I'll do some calculations and I'll give you the card that is the result of all that." Albion swept up the cards.

She looked frightened. "Is something wrong. What's happened?"

He felt confident because he had held the cards. "No, nothing's wrong. Its just that we have to do it again only you have to do it this time. Just the same way as I did it from the shuffle on, just the same way. You're the one who's asking the questions, see, and we've got to get your spirits — I suppose you'd call them — we've got to get your spirits into the cards."

He handed the pack to her. "Now do it, just what I did. And think deeply of yourself, think of what you look like in the mirror and concentrate on what you look like while you shuffle and try to see a light round your face, a sort of glowing ring. Don't be shy. And try to put that spirit you see in your mind down into your arms and your hands."

"But that's not how you do it. I mean I've watched and it's the person who knows all about it lays out the cards, isn't it?"

"It's just the way I do it — otherwise all the spirits would get mixed up. You'd just get me and not you. Go on. I'll tell you what it means. It just tells you where you are in terms of the laws of the universe."

Charlotte shut her eyes, lifted her face and began to shuffle, from her small right hand into her left hand, very evenly Albion noticed, as if she had held a pack of cards in her hands many time. "Now!" She opened her eyes and frowned as she cut the cards, then laid out four in a cross.

"Turn them up."

"Which one first?" He wished that he could see the soft skin of her breasts quivering, as he knew it would be, under her blouse.

"It doesn't matter. Start at the top and go anti-clockwise. Against the sun — widdershins, they call it."

"The Sun too," she said smiling as she turned. Then she blushed for the Devil, smiled for the Star and looked doubtfully at the Chariot. "Now what?"

"I have to find the right card for the middle. It's the result of all the rest." He sorted through the cards until he found Death and put it in the centre of the cross. Boots echoed loudly in the hall. The door opened. Dan stood there. With a shriek of steel he drew out his cavalry sabre and thrust it over them.

"Gotcha! I've got a meeting of the Volunteers. I've saddled up the mare and she doesn't know what she is these nights though she still trots nice and level." He had on a black captain's hat over his black hair and shining eyes. His boots shone round his calves and the gold sergeant's braid glowed in the epaulettes on his tight blue jacket. "They'll get us our proper hats one day — all brass like helmets." He lowered the sword and put it in its scabbard. "Goodnight."

Charlotte was crying. "That card — it means it's all over, doesn't it?"

"Not at all," said Albion in the quiet. "You've got very encouraging cards. Death simply means changing and growing. I'll tell you. Don't cry. You'll see."

"Oh Albion. That was terrible, that Dan with his sword, waving it around. And the Devil. I've got the Devil too, for the card for now. What'll happen to me?"

"Don't forget you're a mother, too. It's not just you in this. I tell you what — it's a bit like an orchard. You know, how you take a scion, a cutting from the tree you want to grow, and you cut a slot under the bark of an old tree root and put the cutting in and seal it with pitch around the wounds and it takes the sap from the old root and grows into a new tree? Well that's the

Tarot, I think. It's about how you can make good use of the things that are happening to you, no matter what they are, so long as you think about them and take the best out of it."

"All right. Tell me, though. Tell me now. I can't get rid of the picture of Dan, of Dan with his sword over us."

It seemed to Albion that the inlaid ivory elephants were moving, moving sun-wise in a circle around the cross, each one holding a tail in its trunk. "Look, everything's changing," he began. "That Death there in the centre, you've got to relate him to all the other cards and Death there is a skeleton." He remembered his thoughts about himself in the bath. "He's a skeleton because that all we're left with, everything else rots away. And he's carrying a scythe which means time and cutting over heads of a boy and a girl and hands and feet which means that our bones are all that's left when our senses are cut off — the tree root, I suppose. So then when you relate that to the Devil, at first you'd think of the Devil's being given to his senses and the fact that impulse makes him work — and see how the man and the woman there are joined by a rope that passes through the anvil the Devil's standing on. I think that means, about your card for the here and now, that you have the chance to leave behind the world of impulse and the senses, things that might have been important to you until now.

"But your future card's the Chariot and you can see that the king in the Chariot is standing under a canopy that's held up by the four pillars of heaven, and the chariot's drawn by a red horse and a blue one, and red and blue make purple which is the royal colour but even though the horses are both looking to the right they seem to be pulling in different directions. Everything's looking to the right too, and I wonder what's over there for them.

"Looking towards something, see, and I wonder what it is

and the king has the face of a man on his left coat shoulder and the face of a woman on his right, looking to the heavens but a load he doesn't feel. But even though he has dominion over everything and gold and great wealth and a sceptre and success, it's still all subjected to change and being swept away by the scythe, even the letters S.M. on the front of the chariot which I think of as standing for Supreme Majesty.

"So your future is great wealth and dominion over material things. But always you are looking into the unknown. Does that sound better?"

"Much better, thank you. But what about the Sun?" She looked relieved and curious.

"They're your thoughts. The Sun with radiant rays — one big one at the top in red and gold and dripping light over two little boys, one touching the other. The red's the colour of the senses and it seems to dominate the picture. It seems to say you think of having another boy but that would be subject to change, too. What do you think about? I'm sorry, I shouldn't ask you when I'm faced with that — a good view of the world. And at the bottom is the Star in fulfillment. It seems to show that you put all your resources into the stream that flows from you as a woman — naked and pouring water from two pitchers to make a stream, everlasting womanhood, it seems, and in that tree on the left there's a bird like a kingfisher which must be going to seek life in the stream. Oh it's good, it's very good, but never forget, it's in the process of changing as time goes by."

"Can you sum it all up?"

Albion was silent. He saw the tear stains on her face. The elephants were still. He knew that he had told her only a little. He felt the presence of many mysteries, of things that he still did not comprehend and that alarmed him. He longed to tell her that it seemed to him to be a good reading. "I don't think

there's much more I could tell you. I'll have to think about it."
He felt reassured at the idea of thought. "Tarot's only a metaphor for the world, I think. It's up to you now. But later on I'll do something more complicated for you and we'll see."

"But if you think it's only make-believe why do you carry a pack of cards about with you?"

"I have a superstitious belief which I regret, as there must be an answer to the riddle of life somewhere and I keep experimenting. I'm testing things — the ancient wisdom idea. I think my mother gave it to me. She entertained gypsies."

"Mother — what are you doing?" He heard Gregory's voice from the door. He was standing there looking in, white-faced in a long pink nightgown. He began to run towards her and she swept up the cards from the table. Destroying the perfect cross, he thought, the cross full of promise. Gregory knelt on the floor and put his skinny arms around his mother's knees.

"But what are *you* doing?" she said. "You should be asleep." She smoothed his hair. "Come on. I'll take you back to bed."

Death," she said when she came back. "Why Death?"

"It was just the numbers," he said. "That was what they added up to. I didn't choose it. You didn't think I chose it, did you?"

Lying in the bath he wished that the water covered him but it just lapped against the middle of his stomach curve. She had said that the water in the stove reservoir would now be hot and that he might as well be the first. He had fetched black iron pots from the scullery and gone into the cool night to fill them at the well. When they boiled on the stove he poured them into the bath, then drew from the reservoir.

It had felt strange to undress into the steam but now he lay back. He thought about the Devil, her present card, and how it seemed neither male nor female, with blue spiky wings over a smiling golden face with hair and breasts which were heavily circled round in black and deeply underlined so that it was impossible to tell its sex, and the dark shadowing in the groin was ambivalent, too. And the image was more than five hundred years old, older than deciding to clothe a man on a horse in a suit of armour, older even than the first cannon. His own sex floated in the water and when he remembered the milkmaid and the milk stain on his thigh he remembered her brown eyes and rose in the water. It was against his will, he thought, wondering about it and then the tear stains on Charlotte's face. Surely the card must say things about her but then they were things that he thought about her himself. He touched himself and his breasts to feel that there were no lines. I am wide open to the Devil, he thought, whatever it is that seems to be within her. But what is the Devil?

He rubbed himself, all over now, and in the folded places of his body, with the rough cake of yellow soap. A ring of scum began to form on the white paint. The well water must be hard. How would he clean it off? He let his neck sink into the water and remembered her dream of pink marble. Finally he sat up, glad that there were no hairs on his chest in which the scum might settle. And the water, when he pulled the plug out, spiralled in a whirlpool widdershins. In the north it went the other way. Could it be that that was the way of the Tarot down here too?

At Lookout Point they stopped. She was wearing a dress of translucent voile embroidered with blue delphinium flowers, some so dark that they were peacock and unreal, an overdress with a dark cream silk beneath. She had let her hair out and had a straw sun bonnet over it.

"We're going down to Brighton to see Henry Jubes at the coal," she had called in the dawn, knocking on his door. Dan said that he wasn't taking his horse down there and had gone to the livery stable, coming back with a heavy bay with big feet that he put between the shafts of the surrey cart for them. On the long heave up the Caversham valley they had said nothing, swaying slowly on the horsehair cushion covered in worn leather, while the iron wheel rims crackled in the road and the horse seemed to pick its way carefully. On each side were little poor houses, some timbered, some of mud bricks with thatched roofs, some merely A-frames stuck on the hillside with chimneys smoking at the back over steep thatches of tussock bound down.

"That's Green Island below there," said Charlotte, gesturing to the south, "where you can see there beside the burn in the rocks. It's got coal and clay and limestone and there's talk of making cement." He could see a few fenced outlines of yards full of drays and carts and ploughs lined up, etched figures in the dark green bush. Below them the road was steep and narrow, winding down to another valley from what seemed a breathless height. "There's talk of a railway now," she said, "out to Fairfield where they're making bricks and tiles, up towards Saddle Hill." And then she leaned against him as they began to go down. "Oh Albion, I feel you know so much about me now."

"You've told me very little," he said. He wanted to hold her hand but she seemed so lithe.

After breakfast at a stable where they changed horses on the cross-roads where the Brighton road began, he was comforted with the smoked fish, the jellied ox tongue and hard-boiled eggs, the scones and jam and tea. The road was straight, over low downs and becoming more sandy, and Dan had put in a chestnut with white feet.

"I didn't think I'd go for Gregory's father at first," she suddenly said. "I was in the grocer's shop on my afternoon half day off and buying something or other and he came in, wanting tobacco, I think. He had a piece of paper with a scrawled list on it. 'What's this say?' he said and thrust it at me. 'Can't you read?' I said, rather prim I thought because he was very handsome, standing there beside me with his bright eyes and black pointy beard. I knew he was a foreigner because I'd seen them about. I was just a servant girl then, doing the washing for a big house. But I could read enough to see that he was after tobacco, lots of it. 'It's for my crew,' he said, and I knew he was off a ship. I was just young, I suppose. I was doing the washing and I'd come out on the ship, seeking my fortune, you know, living in the women's barracks first and being taken on by a gentleman. You had to take what you could get so when Grigori asked me if I'd walk with him I said yes. That was the end of it, really. I was on his ship that night with the little monkeys scrabbling on the deck above my head and that blue lion in the corner of his room. The *Plasma*, the brig was called, after a kind of green quartz jewel, he said, and they'd come out from Bangkok with rice and sago and brass and teak and mahogany for furniture and things like that. Big slabs of bronze, he said, and he gave me one of the monkeys from his rigging later. You've seen it in the yard — and the blue lion, he gave me."

The cart wheels were quieter on the soft road. The horse snorted as they began a hill. She laughed and looked into the overhanging trees. "It didn't take me long, did it. But he was so kind to me even though he said things I couldn't understand. His family had come from Bohemia, he said, and left there to go to Switzerland in the uprisings in 1848 and he went down the Rhine from Basle — that's why he called himself Basle — and went off to sea and travelled the world, he said. He said women only wanted babies and men had to give them to them. He had grown to be all for freedom, he said, after the bad things he'd seen when he was little. He'd get all worked up and wave his arms around. He told me I was pretty and said I was far too pretty to be doing people's washing. He made me just — melt, I suppose. That's what it felt like, and then he sailed away and I've never seen him again."

"But he left you with something good," Albion said.

Then he learned that when she became heavy she had to leave her situation. She took a room in the damp down in McClaggan Street and tried to look after the baby by taking in washing for strangers. Sometimes she was not even able to eat but her figure came back. One day, outside the Renown, an ale house, a woman stopped her in the street. It was Henrietta McPherson, a person she had often seen about there. And gold had been found at Gabriel's Gully and the town had become full of men, shacks and tents going up everywhere and people crowding onto the tiniest bits of land. Henrietta said she must go and make money by pleasing the men.

"She was so kind to me. She said I could pay her back and she gave me a gown, a crinoline. It was poppy red and had a low bodice. She bought me little fine black boots and a satin bonnet. She took me to the girls at Thora's and had Yvonne make me some gloves of poppy red tulle and I met Mavis and Dolly there and Henrietta had them with her too but she said Dolly could look after Gregory as well. Then she told me I had to get a cab and go to the Provincial Hotel one night in all my new clothes and all the gentlemen who had come after the gold were there and drinking whisky round little tables on their plush seats."

Albion moved on the cushion which was beginning to feel hard, and looked across now at the sea. An island stood off the coast, green and yellow with salty scrub.

Charlotte said it had not been long before she was asked to join a table. He glanced at her and could see her leaning forward there in her poppy red, at the table. Henrietta had measured her naked, and told her not to wear stays because she didn't need any pushing up. She was still like that, he thought. "She told me all sorts of ways for not getting pregnant again — washing and vapours from kettles of herbs and things. She even gave me an aquamarine to put under my pillow."

"So then what?" He tried to sound amused. She was talking as if they were somewhere else.

"One thing led to another." She hadn't minded. All she could think of when she took off the poppy red dress was that the crinoline hoops were very awkward, and about damp and being hungry and Gregory. She thought that she would always love his father but she had paid Henrietta her money and she met good men. They would write to her from the goldfields to tell her when they were coming. She met Logan and others who seemed to care about the countryside and seemed to learn a lot from it in some strange way, and early on she met James Lancaster who was getting a lot of gold from his claim and wanted to get into shipping.

"Mr Lancaster kept coming back for me and I had lots of dresses by then that Thora made for me. And Mr Lancaster built that house we're in and then he set off for what he said was his new world. He was very warm towards me then. 'You can have the house,' he said. 'Look after it for me.' He said he would send me money and he does." She finished with all the other men. "I didn't need that any more. I don't even want it."

She sounded anxious and turned towards him at last. "You believe me, don't you. I don't want any more of that kind of life. I've got the house and it's all over and I'm not waiting for Mr Lancaster and I know he'll keep looking after me."

They were moving down, quiet on marly ground, to a wide stream estuary now, with ducks and swans floating, bullrushes standing up with their dark heads and the silver and pink feathery heads of the toe toe standing like idle flags. The early February air was hot and he felt sweat on his chest. She shook her head, took off her bonnet in the sun and fanned herself with it. "The ferry at last."

Beyond the black figure of Dan at the reins and the curved muscles of the horse's silky rump, rope was coiled in the corner of a wooden punt with tarred joints in its broad decking. The horse walked slowly down the slippery corduroy road of pit-sawn logs and led them silently aboard. In the dark water he saw the flash of smelt. The ferry wire stretched and dipped across and Dan jumped down to pick up the rope and pull them over. Albion wished that she would let him talk about himself but the only sound was the hollow knock of the horse propping a hind hoof, and the swish of the wet rope.

"Poor Henry — he has to drive his bullocks on the beach. It's quite hard, he says, and the estuary's very shallow where it comes out down there."

As they struggled round the crags before Brighton Inlet he looked far down into the sea where the black kelp slank in the swell, coldly among peacock foam. Did he belong down there, he wondered, but soon they were across the little flat and splashing through the river ford. A band of blue swamp hens went before them with red beaks cocked back to watch and the white feathers of their rumps blinking in code on the little yellow hill before they reached the long sea terrace that stretched for miles beneath Saddle Hill and on to Taieri Mouth.

If he took away the sea, the double reef on which rollers of the Southern Ocean broke themselves as if in a dance, it was like Dartmore, he thought, where he had gone high to see if he could see the mating of salmon in the creeks below the tarns, salmon come up the western rivers from the Atlantic. It was a mating he had already watched in the high valleys of Yorkshire, above his father's land, and afterwards he went down until he found a stone public house where a dark Celtic girl looked at him sideways and thought that he needed reminding that "Dere be piskies up to' Dartymore an' tidn't good to say dere baint." Later she had lifted her skirts for him in her attic and, laughing, let him smell her as if she were a city girl. Her black hair was shiny and seemed to fall over her mound in rivulets. He found her clean and sweet. In the morning she showed him a rough brass statuette of a gnome-like creature with horns which she said was the god of groves, the god Cernunnos of the Druids, "the very old folk before the chapel came".

Even though the day was still the sea roared on the outer reef, beating like the sway of a pendulum.

"Henry must have gone up the sand and we must have passed him," Charlotte called. The hole of the coal cutting was black on the hill and empty. "But look — the tide's out. We could go on the rocks inside."

Dan stopped a few miles on. "There's a creek up ahead. I'll water the horse and come back for you in a while when I've done it. Take this." He threw down a sack.

Charlotte climbed out and he stood beside her while the cart went off. They walked down through heavy seeds of sedge binding the sand, over cushions of a creeping plant like rough moss, across a patch of tiny red flowers with round petals growing close as if on a lawn among some yellow lights with daisy faces. She kicked the sand in front of him and ran to the first rock pools. A wave wasted itself on the outer reef and he seemed to look up at the spray which might fall on him but was immediately spent and dropping away. Crevices filled with water ran out and he could see limpets, broken shell, round quartz pebbles among strands of weed like necklaces.

She had tucked her skirts up into her underthings, then turned back and watched his hesitance. "I am a land person," he said to himself. "A water person yes, a river person but not a sea person." An abalone shell, washing clean by the sea, gleamed up at him in violent rainbow colours melting together.

"You can take your trousers off, I don't mind. But leave your boots on. I'll soak them in fresh water when we get home."

He rolled his trousers up to his knees but she had gone on, swinging the sack, right at the edge of the surf, he thought, and in great danger where the kelp swirled in deepening cracks, but often bending to pick up or tear off the black and brown mussels, careless of the dripping. Soon he could see the mussels too and began to gather a few, at last trusting that he would not be overwhelmed by the waves. Even their roar seemed less.

"Here," she said, coming up to him. "Look how fat they are." She broke a shell on the rock and pulled the valve apart to show the fish inside. The plump body was puffed and orange with female eggs. "They're good eating. I like the creamy bits best."

They had to wait for Dan. Albion pulled the wet bag, wrenching his shoulder and heavy on his wrist, over the sand, like a turtle coming to nest. He had pictures of her elegant bare legs thrumming to the sea. He could smell the salt like mother-of-pearl. "All the Emperies of spice and Myne," he thought and then he remembered that it was not "all" but "both the India's", and that "My Myne of precious stones, My Emperie" was in Donne's *Going to Bed* Elegy. The mark in the sand was deep.

"I could hardly believe my eyes," Dan said at last. "There was the horse with his muzzle in the water and I looked up the pool and there was a big black crayfish, still as a rock, looking at us. So I creeped up on him and I caught him from behind like a flash and then I thought there must be others so I got a sack and kept going up the pools and turning over the rocks so I got a bag full. Some of them's quite big but I put back the ones with eggs under their tail. That's where they keep them, like little black grapes." He could hear the hard shells scuttling in the sack like the beginnings of crackers.

Dolly said that they used to catch crayfish in the McClaggan Street creek when they got off the first ships at the beginning, and before the water got foul with the town. She emptied the sack into a pot of water on the stove. Henry said he sometimes ran over them with his waggon, and John Wilkes said that Ross Creek was full of them. "There's so many there," he said. "When the men were building the dam for the reservoir up there, they used to roast them on their fires by their tents for their evening tucker."

Charlotte said that they would be ready just after the water boiled. They would turn pink like ordinary crayfish. She washed the mussels with well water in a bucket, scrubbing off the sand, and then she laid them out in a roasting dish, stoked the stove, opened the oven draft and put them in to open in the heat.

It all made a huge family meal in the kitchen, and Dolly and Mavis and Gregory were allowed to sit down there too while everybody used their fingers. Even Thora and Yvonne ripped the meat from the crayfish tails and scooped out the mussel flesh with their thumbs and dipped their fishy fingers in the bowl of warm water Charlotte put out, wiping them on their napkins. Dolly had made an apple pie with fruit from the garden tree, and Mavis had settled Jersey milk in a pan for the cream to float. They skimmed it on to the pie.

Albion, blushing, found himself soon sitting on the edge of Gregory's bed. The boy thumped his head down on his pillow and wriggled under the blankets, his blonde hair falling into a part over his diamond face. Albion read him a story about a large Irish cat who, by means of magic, was also a prince. The cat rode on a white mare, crossed rivers, courted magical princesses who were locked up in caves by giants, and made sure that bad people took draughts of herbs that made them sleep in windmill kitchens.

He blew out the lamp carefully in a room with the moon and stars on a dark paper.

THREE

"We even have a newspaper, I see," he said in the morning kitchen. She was in her brown house blouse and skirt at the kitchen table with the paper spread out and a cup of tea beside her.

"I always like to see what ships are in — who's come and who's dead. It's full of politics all the time, though. So much about the schools and the church and who's going to get leases for the sheep lands out there. The gold's getting further and further away up the rivers and people are always getting drowned. But there's a situation here if you want to work." She pushed a page towards him.

"THE ACCLIMATISATION SOCIETY OF OTAGO.
The Society is looking for the services of a man to supervise the delivery of fertilised Atlantic salmon eggs due to be landed on her arrival from the Celestial Queen, *clipper, departing Gravesend, the Sixth of January* 1868 *and their successful hatching out in a place prepared by the Society's officers and their subsequent release into the Taieri River.*

Accommodation is provided at the site on the Deep Stream. Equipment and stores will be provided by the person appointed. The salary will be St.100 per annum.

Inquiries must be made immediately to the Secretary of the above society."

"But they can't ship fertilised salmon eggs down here. They just go rotten. It's the heat in the tropics — and all the ice melts and the water won't stay cold or it gets poisoned and they've tried other things that swing with the ship but the eggs still get thrown about and they die."

"Well, you seem to know all about it. And they must have found a way to do it. You'll have to make an application. It's the only way to find out. Anyway they're mad about bringing everything from the Old Country out here and getting it started. They say it'll be free food and you won't have to pay for it like the gentlemen do for their fishing and shooting. Or have a right because you own the land."

"Does nobody have a right here then?"

"Nobody. It's all new."

"I'll have to think about it, then. I'll have to write it all down."

On the high moors he had lain at the edge of a stream pool, on his cold stomach in the furze and watched the salmon dance. With a grey sky there was no reflecting light on the water and he could see in — at two fish, a female who was wriggling her body and sweeping her tail to scoop up the bottom gravel until the ridges were about six feet square, squirming and forcing the pebbles aside while the cock fish, long and silver with a detectable pink stripe on its side and a jutting lower jaw hook, sidled by the redd she was making, waiting. Now and then other male fish would come into the circle of his lidless bright eye and he would rush and bite, gripping them at the wrist where their tail began or butting them until the scales were raised.

Patches of white from fresh water fungus painted their skin but the hen and cock were clearly together. They rested a while. A little smolt, a juvenile who had not yet been swept down to the river, flashed in and out across the redd without being fought.

How they bit, he wondered, watching the proud station of the cock and his watchfulness, his readiness to move his full body in defence as she began to move again in her mating spasms. He floated up above her, almost out of Albion's sight through the sedge leaves. A heron flapped, grey and awkward across the pool and settled on the log of a willow up stream. And as he floated she dipped to the red and from her vent the red eggs tumbled. The pool was windless. He saw the cock descend as the hen moved sideways. The white milt clouded from him, colouring the water over the eggs while the smolt, gravely excited, swam in and out, spraying little clouds too. Again and again the hen moved over the redd and the cock jetted down his milt in clouds that drifted slowly in the current but fled first through the glistening mounds of eggs.

He watched motionless for several hours while the fighting and the dancing went on. Then he tried to rise from the sedge and was stiff with cold. The dance would go on, he thought, and in the eggs the little black eye spot would in the end appear. He went on his long walk back to his cottage. Birds flew up from the heather and he wished for his gun. He had never heard talk of such a sight or seen it described. Perhaps he was the first and he would have to try to write it down, but he never did.

He went to his room for pen and paper. Somehow he would have to explain to the Society that he knew about salmon. Their eggs were so tiny considering the bulk of the fish, only about three-sixteenths of an inch across the round. He remembered that, as he walked in Fleet Street in London, he'd seen a crowd of people at the window of a pet shop. They were staring at an aquarium in which salmon eggs lay. Signs said that if passers-by watched carefully each day they would see the eggs start to hatch. He passed for several days and there was always a crowd but the eggs did not hatch for them. Now slowly he began to write, making several beginnings, several 'Dear Sirs', but tearing up the paper and unable to go on. He went downstairs and asked Charlotte if he could dig the garden instead. She said there was a spade and a shovel in the shed by the vegetables.

First he dug a long trench in the untilled ground, feeling the hammer of his instep on the shovel again in his thigh. Christians in the Reformation Church had said that digging was the best cure for low spirits. He rolled up his sleeves, found the wooden wheelbarrow and filled it with manure from the stable dung heap that Dan had piled up. He piled soil from the next trench into the first and then went on, digging and filling and covering, in a kind of dance, he thought, as the bodies swung silver before him and the eggs tumbled and the milt spewed out. Sweat ran into his eyes and down his spine. A bird began to sing in a black beech tree at the corner of the cow paddock. That's a thrush's call, he thought. How can that be? He looked up and could see nothing. The digging went on as if the spade were doing it of itself.

When he had finished he washed the shovel in a bucket of water from the well. He went into the shed to put the shovel away and heard a squeaking chatter behind him. The monkey ran in and began to climb about the piled implements up onto a shelf where wood tools were stacked, then in the dimness down it jumped onto some filled sacks in the corner and began to tug at their folded tops, looking at him. One of the sacks was filled with broken white lumps of rock, slightly greasy with damp. Both were made of hessian sealed with gutta percha latex, and the second was softer to his touch. He opened it and felt damp mud. It was fine and looked black though when he turned to the light he could see that he had a greenish handful. The monkey sang. He put the mud back and closed the sack.

Outside he saw that Gregory had dug a hole with the garden spade the maid had left standing up. He was lying in the freshly turned earth, sighting down a piece of rotting wood from the creek, an imaginary gun. The soil was trampled down around him, a personal redoubt that he had made from which to fire at enemies. He was singing a martial song to himself about a soldier hearing the call of a drum. Albion felt filled with anger that his careful digging had been spoiled before any planting had been done. The sun was hot and the boy's hair shone. It was as if he was not aware of the digger standing there, looking at the ruin of his work. The monkey ran to him and jumped onto the gun stick, wrestling it with his hands. Then it jumped on Gregory's back.

Albion thought that there would be no purpose gained in saying anything. At least if he wrote his letter it would not be trampled on so soon by a boy coming home from school. He rinsed his hands with well water and went up to his room, the sweat suddenly cold on his shirt. He wrote of how he had studied salmon in Yorkshire, of how he had helped gentlemen to catch them and how he had guarded the high streams where the eggs were laid. He wrote of Fleet Street and of how he had travelled in the West Country to see the fishing there and how the wild life gathered in the river valleys. He wrote of his love for wild places and how he could live alone and cook for himself, and of the crowds in Fleet Street, and of the death of his mother and father and how he had used his inheritance to see England and Scotland and travel to New Zealand and how he felt that the new country was full of promise and needed to be filled with the things of Home.

Then he wrote that he was able to rely on himself to discover new things and care for them, that he was a single man of thirty-three years and that he had brought resources with him but wanted to have employment where he could join in, seeing the country and learning about it, of his feeling that he would stay. He had, he wrote, an uncle who was a famous newspaperman in Dublin and was now a rising politician in Australia, and how he had read many books, educating himself, and how he believed in the new science of biology and the thinking of people like Darwin and Huxley and the new discoveries in physics and chemistry and the new ways of engineering and the use of iron in such mechanisms as the steam engine.

He had been brought up in the Established Church by his mother and schooled in an establishment overseen by his vicar, and this he described. He wrote that he had understood the principles of land ownership but that his travels in the cities had made him realise the importance of wild creatures and he would like to see them become a permanent part of the New World. *'Your obedient servant, Albion Duffy, Lancaster House, McClaggan Street, Dunedin. February 16, 1868.'* He would send it straight away by messenger to the Society at its rooms in the new Botanical Gardens building.

Charlotte and the men would look at him as though he were ill-tempered during those days of waiting. Stiffly he kissed Gregory goodnight but did not read to him. He lay on his bed thinking about his old days and about the sacks in the garden shed, about the monkey.

"The trouble with Dunedin," Charlotte said, "is that these Scottish butchers from Aberdeen and Dundee don't know how to make corned beef." She would ask the grocer to bring saltpetre, mix it in water and put large pieces of rolled beef brisket in a tub with it and some molasses. In about three weeks they would be red and ready. "I suppose saltpetre was too expensive for them in Scotland. When I've boiled it and the liquor is cooled, Dolly can take off the fat and it makes perfect pastry for a mutton pie."

Albion thought that he was not even very interested in food. All he waited for, day after day, was a call through the house that there was a post or Dolly knocking on his door to say that a message had come. In the late afternoon he would walk down the path to the Exchange and brood that he hardly knew the town or anybody in it. He had dyspepsia at times and decided that only distraction and motion could relieve him of bis black mood. They seemed to have an effect on the nervous system but were always replaced by the dark urgency of waiting. Sometimes he would hear faintly Charlotte plucking at the piano, one-fingered, he thought, because she had picked up only the rudiments of music and would struggle for what seemed hours to pick out a tune. Then suddenly she would have the full melody of *The Minstrel Boy, Cockles and Mussels* or *The Kerry Dancing*, and once she achieved *Drink To Me Only* and *The Lonely Ash Grove*, even *Just a Song At Twilight* which made him writhe on his bed with a hot feeling of fullness that for a little while took away his despair at ever hearing good news. The salmon eggs were so fragile and tiny.

"I'm sure you need cheering up," Charlotte said one day. He resented that, because it implied that he was in low spirits and he did not want anybody to know that, even though he realised that it must be apparent. "Come across on the ferry to the Vauxhall Gardens with me this afternoon." He dressed carefully, putting on dark trousers and a floppy tweed cap with a peak. He knew that going to the hills of Vauxhall on the other side of the harbour was an occasion and that in being on the Peninsula which protected the port he would even feel a change of climate.

A north-east wind blew as usual down the harbour but lighter than usual. Smoke from the high funnel blustered them at times while the ferry paddles hissed in the water and they had to wipe soot from their eyes. He watched the people and felt an intolerant hatred of crowds and possibility that other people might be going to the same place as they and enjoying every moment of it. The women dressed, like Charlotte, in bright colours under practical shawls, and he thought they would hurt his eyes in the sun coming off the water.

"There's plans to build a swimming baths here," said Charlotte as they manoeuvred stern first into the Vauxhall jetty, below a path leading up the cliff and a ticket office in striped canvas. "Not many people want to swim but the only place for them is off the jetty going out in Lake Logan and they say it's shallow and dirty." She had to shout above the noise of people going off the ferry. "They think they get diseases there — all the illnesses like scarlet fever and measles and diphtheria. They say there's too many fevers in the town and I worry about Gregory."

Albion was not prepared for the jollity of the Gardens. Chinese lanterns, lit even in the day, hung in the trees along the bush walks. He could hear a pipe band in the distance and they passed a shooting gallery, a hammer test in which a powerful man could shoot a weight up a track. A hot air balloon was tethered, tugging towards the sky with a fire beneath it. He saw a dwarf and a very hairy fat lady, bright parrots in an aviary, a booth where women showed bolts of cloth dyed in remarkable colours, a prize-fighting ring where a barker called out that 'Hore' Joe, a heavily muscled Maori with dark tattoos on his face and tight black trousers belted with a silver buckle under his naked chest, was about to fight a bearded ginger man off a farm or a dray. Because it was near Easter there was a diorama through which they could look and see the coloured robes of Joseph and Mary in a stable with a cow eating hay in a manger, and the little Christ that Mary held out to Three Wise Men in blue conical hats.

She touched his elbow. "Do you believe in that?"

"I was brought up to it."

"But I came through so many things on the ship coming out and then I had to do — you know what — and the world seemed very fierce and unpleasant. In the end I don't think I understood it any more, I mean what they were getting at."

"Me too, I suppose. I stopped seeing much goodness in the world. I saw too much of it."

"I don't know how men can call women 'fallen' when it's all their own fault. It's really what they desire that does it, I found."

At the shooting gallery she watched as Albion put a musket ball through a bull's eye and the ginger man's face became broken and bloody while 'Hore' Joe pummelled away with his bare hands. There was the stench of their sweat. They waited for the bell and then moved on past a stage where some men and women and a man with a donkey's head were acting scenes from *A Midsummer Night's Dream* in affected voices, and then saw a rotunda where people were dancing to sounds from a couple of violins, a cello and an oboe. She led him onto the floor and he felt how close she was but did not dare take her hand yet as they walked back towards the ferry, seeing a dark man, weathered and full bearded who was drunk and walking crookedly, singing while he conducted himself with his bottle.

Ma chandelle est morte,
Je n'ai plus de feu.
Ouvrez-moi ta porte,
Pour l'amour de Dieu.

"He looks like he's been mining."

"Yes - but I don't understand what he's saying. It's French, isn't it."

"It's an old song. I think it's something like, 'My tallow candle is dead or gone out and I will never again have any more fire.' Matches, I suppose. Then he's saying 'Open the door for me, for the love of God'."

"That's terribly sad." She brushed his hand with hers.

"I suppose he's lost all his money. I suppose he couldn't even ship out from here if he wanted to."

"I never forgot the first time I got drunk. It was awful. I was going to fall over everywhere in the hotel and I couldn't speak properly. It was Logan Salpetreux who gave me brandy when I usually only had a little wine. But then he was kind and he helped me. I was always careful then."

Fog had come down the harbour and there was a misty rain. It glistened like dew on the shawl she put around her hair as they stood on the ferry deck. Water dripped from his cap. The smoke blew away from them with the wind. "Even though it's autumn it's like spring," he said.

When they got home the letter said:

Dear Mr Duffy,
The appointments committee of the Acclimatisation Society of Otago would be pleased if you would wait upon it in the Botanical Gardens rooms at 7.30 p.m. on Thursday the 15th inst. of March 1868 with a view to considering your application for the Society's position of Salmon Hatchery Manager at its Deep Stream facilities.
Yours etc.

"You'll be all right, I reckon," Dan said when they had driven up the long main streets to the Gardens. "Just be straight with them, I'd say. They can't turn a good man down."

"That's very kind of you. You cheer me greatly."

The buildings were in an open triangle of flat ground where Lyndsay's Creek from North-East Valley joined the Leith. He could see a wooden foot-bridge over the creek to high ground that was being planted out with trees. He assumed the rooms would be at the end of a glasshouse with small white-washed panes which stood before him after he passed around the rushes of a duck pond with water lilies. He was careful of traps set for rats and wild cats which had escaped from ships and the town, and would feast on eggs and chicks. At the door a brick chimney loomed over him. There were seedlings in earthy hessian bags to be planted out — azaleas, pines and larches, cedars and cyprus from Scotland and the islands of Italy and Spain, trays of daffodil and tulip bulbs ready for beds and meadows. A row of oak seedlings stood impressively alone.

Inside the browning white flowers of a rhododendron, an ice queen from the Himalayas, he thought, lay on the stone flagged floor. He opened a further door in a wave of heat. Steam pipes from the boiler ranged around a room full of begonias with pink faces, dripping water fuchsias, tropical orchids, yellow and bronze in hanging sprays around a banana tree, maidenhair fern in clay pots. Through a further door it was cool. He knocked.

The room was sparse, chairs drawn up around an oval kauri table, men in high jackets with winged collars over silk ties. Papers littered the table and the cigar smoke was thick. He was conscious of his soft collar under his tight jacket. He stood, trying to be straight and wanting to sneeze. He tried to put names to the faces which all seemed plump and not creased. Perhaps that was James Hector, the Provincial Geologist who had started his career as a geologist and explorer after obtaining a degree in medicine because that was the only science in which Scotland gave degrees.

Maybe that was Julius Vogel who was in politics and was one of the owners of the newspaper — a man of foresight who, it was known, wanted to write a novel about women as they might be when the Second Millennium came to pass, who believed in Great Britain and colonisation and thought, resentfully, that the South Pacific was being neglected by the Empire. He had studied chemistry and metallurgy but was unfortunate in business enterprises. Albion thought this man seemed to have forgotten that the lands he wanted colonised had become Christian because the British Christian missionaries had tied up the brown people and flogged them or had them killed with gunpowder.

They seemed all to be members of what the town's founders, the Reformed Church of Scotland, called 'the New Iniquity.' Englishmen or those committed to English ideas, a kind of cabal of men who would say they were 'from the Enlightenment' and would claim political influence. A thin man with an intent face and wire spectacles was probably the naturalist.

There was a sea of faces but he picked out the person he thought was the chairman before they became blind to him again — a man wearing an old-fashioned white stock instead of a tie, stuck with a large turquoise, who began by saying, "Let me tell you about our Society's aims, Mr Duffy. We formed ourselves so that the sportsman and lover of nature might enjoy the same sports and studies that make the remembrance of our former home so dear, so that the country will be rendered more enjoyable, our tables will be better supplied and new industries will be fostered. We are devoted to these objects."

Then the questions came at random before he could identify the speakers. He could not split them up into individual pictures but that, he supposed, was the way of inquiry. The most important thing he could do was to spill out, sweating, the

THE BLUE LION

thoughts with which he had laboured for years.

"Can you tell us what you know of science?"

"I know that the earth turns round and that it also goes around the sun. And that the sky is blue because dust is trapped in the air and reflects the light. It's a very big question, Mr Chairman." Perhaps he had been impertinent. He could only hope that they would persist with him. His collar was wet and his face felt swollen, his mouth too dry.

"Well said. And tell us — what do you think have been the most important advances in science? And I should include engineering there."

"I'd say first of all it was gun powder, and then the telescope and the microscope, and the Bessemer converter for making lots of steel from iron."

"But other discoveries have been pertinent to advance, what has been called the march of minds."

"You would have to include the micrometer for measuring things accurately but before that mathematics in metres and not feet and inches. That would bring us to the forces of gravity and electricity and magnetism that bind the atoms that things are made of tightly together and the elliptical courses they are in. And there's the miner's safety lamp which depends on chemical reactions and the behaviour of gases, how they move and combine — the spiral and the parallel line. And acids and alkalis and oxygen in air causing rust and all of us being dependent on oxygen and the way plants make green stuff out of sunlight and air. And what happens in fire."

"Then what is time?"

"Time seems to be just the space between two things that happen."

"And what about animals and the way life seems to be organised?"

"I believe in what Mr Darwin says about the origin of species and natural selection. We can learn much from bones and studying the past. Many discoveries have been made. It's even said that rodents with warm blood caused the dinosaurs to be extinct because they bred so fast and ate all the reptile eggs."

"And what do you think about breeding, Mr Duffy?"

"I've been convinced by Dr Malthus and the notion that there will keep on being more and more men until there isn't enough food and then there'll be a revolution and a lot will die and we'll go back to the beginning."

"What about the microbe, Mr Duffy?"

"The study of the single cell has proved that microbes are in the air and will grow in anything liquid and that they will cause sickness if they are not killed by chemicals or heat or cold. Miss Nightingale has recalled that in the Crimean War the propeller of the little steamer sent to give aid to our soldiers turned up rotting bodies in the harbour wash at Feodosiya, I think it was."

"What about their consciousness of light?"

"Our eyes are the first organs we grow — you can see that in the salmon eggs. First of all they have the black eye spot and you know they are fertile. They grow in darkness. I don't know about microbes, I'm sorry." That seemed to be his first admission of ignorance. He felt more relaxed but what would they think of him now?

"And people, what do you think have been the most important things to happen to people in the fairly recent past?"

"I would say the abolition of slavery and the abolition of child labour in the factories and mines and the repeal of the Corn Laws and changes to the vote."

"Do you approve of the repeal of the Corn Laws?"

"I've been a working man, sir, even though my parents had land. I've wanted the price of bread to come down just like all working men."

"What about the Church, Mr Duffy?"

"We are all God's creatures, sir, and the Church is there to help look after them. The Church does fine work in helping the poor and giving them hope and in looking after the sick. To my mind, that is where it does best. But I think a room must always be made for experience of the mystic and ecstatic — man's sense of union with God."

"And what about acclimatisation — that is our purpose, after all," the chairman said.

"It's a matter of latitude. Things that flourish in the north in a particular latitude should flourish at the same latitude in the south. It seems to me we should try to do that."

"You seem to be very well informed, Mr Duffy," the naturalist said.

"Thank you, Mr Duffy. We will make our decision known to you."

"I don't know if I was impertinent or said to much. They seemed a tough bunch of men but kind, I thought. I feel bleak now," he said to Dan as they drove slowly back to Lancaster House. He sat high beside him on the hard driver's cushion. "I didn't even talk to them about railways and steam. I didn't even tell them we could take the eggs to Deep Stream in the brougham if that was all right with you and you had the front seat mended. And all my gear. Oh what a pickle! Just more waiting." He was being childish, he knew, but he had done his best. "I tell you what," he said suddenly, amazed at the resilience of his mind. "Those sacks of rocks and mud in the garden shed. Do you know what they are?"

"Charlotte's had them for years. Logan gave them to her."
"But what's in them?"

"It's some stuff he found when he was prospecting, she told me. He went away up to the Wakatipu region when the Rush started there — to the Shotover, I think. And he brought those back on his horse, in his saddle bags. He even made her maps of where he dug them up."

"But what are they?"

"I don't really know but apparently he said that the mud stuff was very ancient and left by the glaciers that scoured the earth up there. It was all the dead bodies of things killed by the ice and dropped down. He said it would be like a mud pack. She could put it on her face. Fancy that. And it would peel off and take away the wrinkles. You know how women get about things like that. But she never tried it, I don't think. Not that I ever saw her. And the rock stuff — that would have to be ground up and make some kind of salt to put in the bath. It would make the water soft and be good for the body. Tone it up, he said. They get it somewhere in Germany or Austria. And in England too, I think. But she's never had a bath to try it.

"Logan was a queer fish. He knew a lot about different kinds of rocks, never mind the gold. He made a fortune at that too and then he went off and she started seeing Lancaster whenever he came down."

"Maybe they're worth something then," Albion said, and felt his head go light. Rocking behind the horse made him feel dizzy and even the moon that was coming up behind him, over North-East Valley, did not seem to heal him.

FOUR

"His name means something like 'Fat boy looking at the moon, smiling'", she said, "or that's how I think of it and I want you to meet him." She had on a deep red blouse with leg of mutton sleeves, high collar and red glass brooch over a matching red linen skirt. "Actually his name's Elegant Cheng or something like that. He was the first to start a restaurant here and somehow I helped him along because it was our street."

"Your red stone," he said. "It's like my birth stone or what they tell me it is. A garnet."

"Capricorn. I'm Scorpio. Henrietta always said it was aquamarine. But I think I told you that — about putting it under my pillow."

"It's what your Tarot cards say." He was easier with her now in spite of the waiting. She told Dolly that they would be out for supper.

"Fat Boy came and asked me for help," she said as they walked down the street. "That was very unusual, I thought, but he wanted to get the miners to eat at his place. They came from all over and they were used to Asian food or that's what he worked out. But it was the decoration he was worried about — something that would appeal to foreigners. That's how he thought of us. He couldn't even speak much English then but it came into my head that though he'd have to have oil cloth on the tables he could have rocks and things and — the world."

They could hear the sad sound of a violin playing inside. "In spring the worm produces silk until it dies." Fat Cheng seemed to be saying immediately, standing at the entrance with a canvas apron. "This is what olt person say, Miss Charlotte. I hope you be very happy." She had had the words 'Wan An' painted on the door and some Chinese characters. "It means something like a thousand blessing on your night. He's very well read as well as being a good cook. He always greets me like that — with something ancient. When I think of what these people have done for our goldfields — I felt I owed them so much."

There was a moss-grown stone tumble inside with water trickling down from a spigot in a wooden bucket at the top. The violin was louder. She had papered the walls in the same dark blue with stars and moons as Gregory's bedroom. In a corner was a lacquered space with joss sticks and ivory statuettes and a silk picture of a bird among piney crags. "That's their space — " she nodded to several men sitting at the tables, a mixture of men of the town and miners with rough clothes and shaggy beards, their elbows on the tables. A few young women sat with them in low dresses and bright colours.

"The ships bring what they need from China, all the way down the coast. There are things like dried mushrooms and sesame oil and bamboo shoots in jars and beans to make sprouts and special herbs and powders. I'm always amazed at the flavours and its all mixed with smoke from the men's cigars. That reminds me that I do hope Mr Wilkes is all right. He said he had to go down the harbour towards Port Chalmers to see how they would fill in lines across the bays for the railway to run on. Later on you'll see the girls get up and dance round the tables. I hate that violin but I told Cheng that the men would want it. Tell me more about the Tarot."

Her change was so sudden that he felt threatened. He put off replying and asked if they could order food instead. "The chicken and pork are always good," she said as if she had noticed his hesitance. "There's always plenty of meat and the batter is really crispy if that's what you want. I don't use chopsticks, by the way. I have to ask for a fork."

When the food was before them he said, "The point about your Tarot seems to be your birth sign, I think."

"How would that be?"

"Well you're Scorpio according to your birth sign in the stars. And your cards added up the other day to the Death card. When is your birthday?"

"November the second." Steam from her plate misted her glass brooch.

"That means that your Tarot card is the six of Cups."

"Is that good?"

"It means the beginning of pleasure. It's ruled over by the Prince of Cups and that's a young man with brown hair and eyes who is — let me see — subtle, violent, crafty and artistic."

"But that's Grigori!" She leaned back with her hand to her mouth and her fork askew.

"He's powerful for good or evil." He felt a strange mixture of power and dislike rising in him, as if he knew that he was trying to make her think what he wanted her to but was unable to stop it. "But in turn he's ruled over by the Princess of Cups. She's a young woman with brown hair. She has sweetness and kindness. She's dreamy and she likes to be lazy. But if she's aroused she's very courageous. She can be selfish and luxurious if she's treated the wrong way."

"Oh I hope that's not me, that last bit."

"And over all," he said, suddenly triumphant, "there's the Ace of Cups and that sums up all the power of what I s'pose you'd call loving-kindness." He sat back, as if he had reached the right conclusion after an ordeal.

"I tell you very olt poetry I learn." Fat Cheng was standing beside them. "Can listen now, please? It go. I have learned in English words, 'A pot of wine comes inside with all flowers and I am by myself when I pour. So I lift up wine and moon is bright. It make me and shadow of me. That makes three people all together.' You like that?"

Charlotte and Albion found themselves laughing up at him out loud and the violin began to play a polka rhythm. Two of the girls got up to move around the tables of men. "More than thousand year olt," Cheng exclaimed. They said that the food was very good.

Albion felt determined to ask questions. "Those sacks in the garden shed. I asked Dan about them. He said Logan Salpetreux gave them to you. But I don't understand what they are."

"Oh, Logan was French. He was very full of words. He would say that the miners only looked for gold in water — alluvial gold, he said it was. But he said that much more gold was imprisoned in rocks, in the reefs of quartz that could be found. He said all that gold could be released by adding the right chemicals when the rock was crushed up. They would combine with the gold and then you could separate them later. Those rocks in the sacks and that mud — he said they were worth much more than gold if you used them in the right way."

"Perhaps we can find out how to use them, then," Albion said.

There seemed to be a fire between them now, Albion thought as they walked back up the hill, and recognised his own sadness that it was about the things they had talked about.

A letter was delivered at last, saying:

"It is my pleasure to inform you that the Committee has decided to offer you the appointment of Hatchery Manager at the Deep Stream station.

"The Committee would be pleased if you would work with its Naturalist, Mr George Henty, if you are willing to accept the appointment. Mr Henty will provide you with all necessary future instructions if you wish to accept the appointment."

There was something deeply satisfying to him in knowing that he had something to do.

Henty was like a great, grey stork, he thought when he went to the Gardens.

"Come and look at this," he said. Albion followed him, almost running behind, as they walked across the grass to a little wooden bridge over Lyndsay's Creek. Across the boards, rocks and clay had tumbled down onto the track. Grass grew tall there.

"Look at this." Henty bent to a flower like a marigold but daisy white. "It's got a blue centre — organs of propagation." The daisy centre was royal blue within a fine black circle. "Now all the daisies I've seen in New Zealand have had yellow centres. Why should this one be blue? What's happened here? Has this plant escaped from some collection from another country? Or is it something that's just grown here and changed for some reason as the pollen has blown about?" He looked worried. "It's certainly a most unusual colour. You know about salmon eggs, I believe."

"I've spent a long time watching them made and seeing them

grow. I've seen them hatch out and looked after the little fish."

"Well, its all a new science, getting them across the tropics into the southern hemisphere. We know they keep growing in the dark. They don't need light at first. That's interesting. But two things kill them once they're fertilised. They will be killed by shock — a blow or a sudden movement. And they need a temperature less than forty-two degrees. Any hotter and they die."

"What I can't understand is how they are bringing them here."

"Very good question." Henty picked the daisy. "Damn. Shouldn't have done that. It might be the only one." He sat down on the bank. "Warm, isn't it? Think there might be rain? We have to thank Mr Youl. Back at home he did experiments. He made boxes of ordinary deal — eight inches square and five inches deep. At the bottom he put a layer of charcoal. Then he put a layers of ice chips, then a layer of living moss. He put the eggs on the moss and covered the lot with ice again. Then he put on the lids. They had to be carefully screwed down because hammer and nails would shock the eggs."

"Why the charcoal and the moss?"

"He thought some eggs would die. They would rot and the charcoal would absorb the gas they gave out. The moss was living and would help keep the eggs alive, as well as being soft. He got ice from the Lakeland Ice Company which made it specially for him."

"Will it work?"

"We'll just have to see — and hope. The boxes were to be put down deep in the hold of the *Celestial Queen* and covered with more ice and wooden insulation. She's due soon."

"I can help, I think. Where I'm living we've got a brougham. We could take the boxes up to Deep Stream about as fast as anything. And its fairly well sprung, or it looks like it."

"That sounds like a good idea — better than relying on the public coach service. Keeping them cool — that's the secret."

"Gregory's got coloured chalks," Albion said suddenly.

"What's that got to do with it?" The stork stood up.

"Oh, I'm sorry. I was thinking of the blue daisy — and the boy where I'm living."

"Let's stick to eggs, shall we? I'll get a message to you when the ship's off the heads."

At home Albion found two pieces of his writing paper and asked Gregory for chalks. At the kitchen table he coloured a band of blue-green down the left hand side of the paper, then, with a space, a column of black, then a column of yellow. He held the paper up to the boy.

"Look at that. Really stare at it for a while." He could hear his mother's voice. Quickly he put down the paper and held up a blank sheet. "Now stare at that."

"But the colours are all different — one's red and the middle one's white and the other one's blue. How did you make them change?"

"I didn't. Your eyes did. That's what eyes do."

What colours would the salmon see, he wondered, in the black eye that was the first form in the red, round egg? The hairs in his nose tingled but there was no wind outside. The fact was that both he and Henty had seen that the centre of the daisy was blue, in its ring of white petals, and not yellow. He had seen it and other eyes had too, at the same time. Surely that was proof.

One afternoon when he came into the kitchen, Gregory sat at the table with a dish and an old clay pipe.

"It's just an old thing of Mother's. And Dolly made me some soap. She's got some in the scullery and scraped it into a pot." He dipped the pipe in the dish of soap and blew a small bubble.

It floated away and burst.

"Let's make that better." He put some sugar from the dresser into the dish and stirred it with his finger. "Now try it," and the boy dipped again and blew. The bubble was large and floated away across the room, falling, coloured in red, orange, yellow, green, blue, indigo and violet in the late sunlight.

"It didn't burst. How's that?"

"The sugar means it doesn't dry so fast, I think. I tell you what — get a piece of paper." Gregory ran off and came back with a piece of writing paper. "It's Mother's again." He handed it and looked away. They heard the monkey scratching at the door. Dolly stood stirring a pot at the stove.

"I'll let him in — just for a little while. He likes to be with people."

The monkey chased bubbles as Gregory blew them, dancing across the floor and leaping up, sitting down with an expression of bewilderment and loss when the bubbles burst. Albion held the paper to the stove. Dolly glanced at him as he stood beside her and said nothing. One bubble was blown up and stuck to her pale hair. Albion took the hot piece of paper to the table. He rubbed it hard with his tweed sleeve.

"Blow me a bubble — blow me two or three and let them rest on the table."

When he held the paper over the bubbles they changed shape from round to oval. Then, when he held the paper closer over them they danced like the monkey. Each time he lifted the paper away so that the bubbles did not stick to it.

"How's that happen?"

"It's electricity. I put electricity in the paper when I rubbed it and that made the bubbles dance."

"Can I do it?" said Gregory as the bubbles burst.

The next day he came from school with his slate. On it,

contained on the black surface and within the rough wooden square, he had written the word 'capture' in uneven little letters.

"We learned a new word today," he told Albion. "It means to catch somebody in a net or make them stay still with a knife or a gun."

Albion did not know what to say. It seemed to him that the word meant much more than that. He had seen the red fire in Charlotte's dark hair. He told Gregory to fetch a stool and place it against the wall. "Now stand with your feet apart, about the same space as the chair is wide. Lean your head against the wall. Pick up the stool and now try to stand up straight." Gregory could not stand straight like that. "You're captured, see. Your own body can capture you. I couldn't stand straight either if I did that." His mother had taught him this old party trick against the cottage wall. He remembered his warmth and wonder, his bafflement at it.

"It's Henry's bath night," Charlotte said as they took tea that night. "He smells all of bullocks and hay."

The lamp light — it was getting dark now at this time — shone on Henry's bald head and in his sparse blonde whiskers.

"There's a fresh soap and a towel out for him," Mavis said, although she was usually silent standing by the tea table. "And Dolly's put all the pots of water on the stove and it's all stoked up."

'Logan's rocks," Albion said. "Will you take an experiment, Henry?"

"Depends what it is, I s'pose."

Albion brought in some lumps from the sack in the garden shed, stumbling a little with his hands full.

"You'll have to put some of this in the bath water, that's all Henry." He looked down at the rocks. "I wonder if they ought to be ground up."

"Whatever they are, if you grind them up they'll be scratchy on my bum," Henry said.

"Why grind them up at all?" John Wilkes said. "If there's anything good in them it'll come out when they're whole, I'd say. The hot water would do it."

"And then I could know where they are in the water," Henry said. "I'd be much happier about that, if you don't mind."

They waited in the kitchen until he had finished and come out in a clean shirt and trousers. "I tell you what — there's something in those rocks. They all melted down. They lost all the rough edges and the water felt light and soft and the soap lathered up beautiful. The water felt all slippery on me. It was good."

"That's just what Logan said would happen. There was some sort of salts in there, he said. Now we've found out about it."

"Maybe people would pay money to have it," Wilkes said in the sudden quiet. "Is there any more of it?"

Charlotte looked as though she were a long way away. "I've got a map," she said. "He left a map with me. It's away up towards the Shotover River, near Lake Wakatipu. That's where the mud came from too, at Skippers." She seemed to be talking to herself.

When on April 16 the *Celestial Queen* was reported standing off and on the harbour heads waiting for a favourable wind with the tide, Henty called Albion to him, absolutely sure that the eggs would have safely made the tropical crossing and talked about the things he would need to take to Deep Stream. At an outfitters in Princess Street he bought an axe, a mattock, a shovel and a spade. He bought a hammer, long nails and chisel. Then he bought half a dozen grey blankets with red bindings, two oil lamps, their fragile chimneys carefully wrapped, and a supply of tallow candles, tins of matches, a lantern with a bull's eye to

— 72 —

focus a beam. There were pots and pans, basins and iron buckets, tin plates and mugs and two table knives, forks and spoons although he was not sure that he would have any guests. He bought a stone bottle for hot water to put in his bed, woolly shirts, socks, jumpers and underwear, some airy calico cloth to make a meat safe and to stop sweat on the side of bacon he bought from the grocer. There were potatoes, flour and rice to buy, oatmeal and small sacks of sugar and salt, raisins and currants, some bottles of jam, a cast-iron camp oven with a lid, and a mincer to grind up cooked sheep liver for fish food.

Charlotte gave him a black greatcoat, a muffler, mittens, woollen hat — an oilskin jacket with sou' wester and a big cape of the new mackintosh material which smelled strongly of rubbery rot but would keep him dry.

In the end he thought that he had assembled everything he needed, even bandages and a bottle of the new 'carbolic' that would kill microbes, and powders for his stomach and bowels.

They went again to the Wan An for a late dinner. "'The victorious army first secures its victory and then seeks battle, while the losing army first fights and then seeks victory'," said Cheng at the door. "I have learned this to say carefully. Me think sound right."

"*I* think," said Charlotte, tall beside him in her black cloak and bonnet with a turquoise lining, all against the cold which had come with the autumn. They ate duck which she said had been trapped on lagoons on the Peninsula but Cheng told them had been fattened in his own yard. The men there looked like seamen and drovers, Albion thought, as the girls moved about.

"I get message from me sister. She still in Canton. She have baby. It call 'Sau Yuk'." He laughed. "That sound mean also 'lean meat'. I think baby not like that. I think it mean 'elegant jade' which smooth. Plump too. Name like me. It is 'elegant', name like me."

"You are very lucky," Charlotte said. The violin was playing a polka again, a sea chanty, *Oh You New York Girls*, loudly and insistently, and he began to wonder about her again as she leaned forward in her beige silk blouse with its pale cameo brooch at the throat. She closed her eyes and they disappeared from him so that for a moment he felt anxious and threatened. He could see inside himself suddenly and his mind felt crowded with colours, things that were growing and physical work, the eggs that were coming.

"I s'pose I shouldn't ask this — but what's it like — having a baby?"

"I don't mind a bit." Her eyes were open and looking around. "You ought to know — I was an orphan. I was a Scouse, a Liverpool Irish girl. I was only twelve when I went to Stow-on-the-Wold north of Oxford. The woman was a piece-worker, making gloves, and I did the washing for the house. The country was very green with the rooks in the trees. So I went when they wanted girls for the settlement here. The doctors said I had good hips and they were taking more than the Scottish girls by then to travel all the way out here. I was fifteen and I had no money then and it seemed the best way."

Albion felt thwarted by this account. She seemed to be answering his question as if he had asked something quite different. "But babies," he said in a low voice.

"I didn't mean to have a baby, not then. I always thought I would sometime — *knew* I would, I s'pose. But it felt grand. At first I didn't care when they found out about me. I felt so good. And then they started to notice. It was the women first. They all seemed to nod at each other when I walked by and I began to worry if I would feel sick but I didn't. And Grigori had sailed away. So I had to wait by myself but I was used to that, even living in a little room down here by myself where it seemed wet all the time. But something was going in me. I still felt grand. I didn't notice things then."

"How did you get on?"

"Well I'd saved a little bit and Grigori left me some money. And then I had to get the midwife and a girl she brought to wipe my face when I screamed. I screamed a lot, I think, my face being wiped with water in a basin beside me, and then it was out and I felt — oh I remember it now. I loved that baby and I felt as though all the good things in the world were happening to me. Everything was bright and I wanted to sing. I washed him and cuddled him and I wanted to sing."

"So you fed him."

"I loved feeding him. I loved having plenty. It seemed, even in the cold, that I'd always have plenty and when he fed from me I felt a tingling all over."

"But it didn't go on?"

"Oh it went on all right but I got thin and my clothes and things were all worn out and my blankets were thin so we had to cuddle up together and I could only have porridge to eat, not even bread, and then Henrietta came along." She looked away again. "And then I started to get all this." Her hands seemed to caress the walls.

"Weren't you worried about fevers?"

"I kept clean. I knew you had to keep clean. That's what I'd done, keeping clean. So nothing bad seemed to happen. I would boil things. And I would sing. That's what it felt like. That's the main thing. All the pain passes away."

Albion felt that she had spoken something he would not be able to understand. He had never been told that women could say things like that. But then, he supposed, he had never thought to ask.

He stood on the tarred wharf looking down at the water which was dark green, reflecting the ship's painted iron hull, its coolness. Henty, Hector and Vogel stood beside him. Cargo had been hoisted from the hold by the jump yards and tackle. They could go on board, he following them up the narrow gangway, looking back to see Dan pulling up with the laden brougham, deftly wheeling the four horses until they were facing the way they would go, wet withers in the early morning.

He wrote holding the pen with the tip pointed at his shoulder, as his mother had said, his wrist raised clear of the paper.

DEEP STREAM
APRIL 18, 1868

Dear Charlotte,
I am already making a sort of home here — there is even a mouse scuttling by the fireplace. They must have crept over the grass from town. I am only 45 miles out but it feels like I am writing to China. I've got my letter case on the table and the chair is rough but I'm warm and the eggs are in the water.

Dan stopped the horses half way down the hill and it was so quiet, not even a lark yet in the endless hills and all the rocks carved out by the wind. Sheep everywhere — McIvor runs more than 40,000 on his station. He wasn't there at the ship. They said he was in Wellington where he sits in the Parliament for Caversham. Barclay, his manager, met us as we came along the stream flat. He was scything away at his front lawn, a scrawny man with bright eyes, no collar over his striped shirt and an open waistcoat. Stubble. He lives here with his wife and with Mary, Dr McIvor's daughter, and her companion and the cowman who does the vegetables and kills the meat and some shepherds. The house is fair, mud bricks and high gables with timber from the nearest big bush at Outram. Chimneys. Washing lines out the back — I kept looking for the monkey! — and the shearing buildings, butcher's shed, cow byre and such beyond up a bit of a slope. Little roses and trees beginning.

My place — I call it that — is a hut that even has a little window with four panes, that still stands on skids as if it was hauled here from somewhere else, a shepherd's hut but the chimney is sound and good. Dan bunked here on the floor with the coach cushions and a couple of blankets I gave him. He put his head on a sack of tea. My bed is a kind of wooden trough in a corner with jute wool sacks stretched across the bottom. The mattress is lumpy, with cotton waste filling and not stabbed properly to keep it on place.

Down there in the ship's hold was still cold, thank God, and all among the dust and old bits of timber they lifted off the wedges of coverings over the boxes of eggs. They were stacked about five feet square and five feet high, still damp even after three months of coming out. Henty unscrewed the first box and we saw the little red eggs gleaming up. Some were yellow and dead, of course, but about half were still fresh. There were big sighs all round. Henty opened another case which was similar — there were cases for 2,500 eggs in all originally. They swung down a hatch cover and we loaded them on. What struck me, in the officers' quarters we looked at, was all the cages. Hector said the Society was bringing in birds. There were cages of larks and thrushes and blackbirds, green finches and chaffinches, yellow hammers, even sparrows and starlings. They said the robins had died which is a pity because I always admired them. Big bunches of seed on branches hung about but I don't know what they did for worms and insects.

There is even a crazed old glass here — I forgot to buy a mirror — and some chipped plates. Of all things there is a toasting wire, some bent pieces on a long handle to hold a slice over the flames. Beside my hut there is a kind of covered race. The stream carved big hollows and left an old meander on a green flat. Water is let in to fill the race ands the ponds and let out again at the bottom with a wooden lock covered with fine iron grating to keep the fry in. It took Dan and me most of the day to lay the eggs out on slabs of schist under the water. The mica gleamed like gold in them. My hands went white with cold. But now they all seem safe in running water and I will just have to wait for the hatching. Hector and Vogel wished me luck at the wharf and said they believed I would do a good job. I had to forgive them for their high coats and top hats. Time flies.

There is little timber about — groves of trees and shrubs with names I don't know yet. There is a broadleaf which yields good wood for the fire. I will be sparing with the coal. There is soot everywhere anyway. Tomorrow I will find a corner outside and plant the tarragon root I have brought all the way from England. In the spring I'll put in seeds for the herbs. I hope they will be still alive after long passages with many storms. I have been amazed how well things grow, though. On the flat plains we came across before we forded the big river I saw hawthorn hedges with red berries, limes and sycamores, elms and horse chestnuts and macrocarpa beginning to grow. Along the river there was even willow which will grow like a weed if they are not careful — I know because I have had to clear many a salmon pool for the rods. There was even a little cemetery. I will explore the stream and tell you more later. Barclay will lend me a horse to get about, a big grey cob he pointed out.

He signed it with his love. He could still feel the ship lurching slightly and hear the grinding of the coach wheels on the gravel roads, the straining of the horses up long tussock hills. That morning he had walked half a mile up to the station house to see if he could get milk. He swung a billy while sun rose on the yellow walls. Just before he knocked on the back door he glanced in the scullery window. A girl stood there with a dripping flannel at her breasts. Water hung on her nipples, out on the creamy skin, the pores of her flesh. It was like looking at a picture in a magazine. He stood very still, having to watch with all his manhood engaged in it, at the picture that she made while he blushed and was unable to stop. Her colours swarmed in him like bees and desire overwhelmed him.

Mary McIvor — it must be her — was clothed at the door, welcoming, he thought, a tall girl with blonde hair loosely caught up, a slightly receding chin, innocent eyes, long pale hands held out for his empty billy, knowing immediately what he had come for.

He rubbed his eyes, dried his pen, shifted the lamp to the edge of the table and stood up to stretch and tend the fire. He thought ruefully to himself that a letter was only as honest as the trickery, the treachery and lies that went into it. In the morning he would ride the grey cob up the hill, over the miles, to put it in the box the coach would clear in a day or two. He felt surrounded by narrow views.

Dan, before he drove off, had sat holding the reins in his high seat, looked at him and then looked away up the stream. A white heron was standing in the reeds at the edge of the pond, an image of the preying beasts he would have to fight.

"The trouble is," Dan said, with his eyes wide out over the hills, "the trouble is you've got to play Charlotte — you've got to play her like a fish." Then he clicked the horses.

FIVE

LANCASTER HOUSE
APRIL 25, 1868

Dear Albion,

There's so much you didn't tell me in your letter that I've been asking Dan for the details again and again. You didn't mention the bacon and egg pie I gave you for victuals to start off with or the loaf of bread. I got the bread specially for you. Dolly made the pie pastry and I filled it. Some people stir up the eggs to put them in the pie but I always prefer to leave the yolks whole. I think it looks better, don't you?

And you did not mention saying goodbye at the gate. I felt so sad because you were going away and I know that Gregory misses you already, with your tricks he doesn't know about. Even Tiny misses you, I think. You are so brave to go off into the wilderness with those eggs and expecting that they will hatch after coming all this way over the sea. I wanted to kiss you goodbye but Dan was there.

You must tell me about the place and what it is like being there.

You sound warm and comfortable. Will you be able to get meat and milk and eggs from Mr McIvor's house? It will be a lonely life for you.

I am thinking of taking piano lessons. There is a woman come here who can teach and has put a notice in the paper. It would do me good to learn to play better, do you think? I love singing so much and I lose patience with myself for being so slow at the piano. I love the sounds that can come out of it if I can do it properly. We have got the apples and pears in off the little trees in the garden and they will keep in the cellar or they have in other years. I will try to preserve some. Here is a recipe for pears. It seems very elaborate: To every 12 lbs of pears put in 12 lbs of sugar and soak for six days. Strain the syrup and add 1 lb of whole ginger crushed. Boil for two hours and take the ginger out. Add the pears and boil for two hours until clear, then prick the pears with a silver fork before you bottle them and put them away while hot. I think I will try that and there'll be some for you at Christmas.

How far away that seems. Do write to me again. I would be very gratified. Your Charlotte."

What did she mean by that, he wondered? He slung his long knife in its leather sheath on his belt and went out to pick up the axe. There was a stand of old manuka close by and he would fell half a dozen trees for winter firewood. They crashed from him as he felt his muscles firm with the axe. A little green gecko ran out from the fallen branches. He wrote straight back.

DEEP STREAM
APRIL 25, 1868

Dear Charlotte,
While I am pleased to have the recipe for pears I fear I will have to go without such delicacies. The day here has been clear with little

wind and I can hear the sheep out in the tussock. It is a wild land. Dr McIvor has 20,000 acres here, over the Lammermore hills, and runs 45,000 sheep. It is much like my home country of north Yorkshire and I suppose that's why they have thought salmon might start here. The road to the Dunstan goldfields lies close by and there is still the occasional waggon over it. I stop my work and watch. The eggs are safe on their stones in the running water which comes in a cutting from the Stream. They will take about 20 days to hatch, I think, and that time is already nearly half done. Then the little fish will live for about 21 days on their yolk sacks at their heads. Then I will have to grind up boiled liver to feed them. Many dangerous birds stalk round the pond and I have seen eels that could eat them.

Yes, I do remember saying goodbye. It would have been good to embrace you, I think — but I mustn't go down that road. You have been so kind to me and yes, we did enjoy the pie and I toasted some of the bread on my fire and had it with the jam you sent. I have been getting in firewood and discovered the privy. I had not thought there was one here but it is tucked away in some old beech trees and looks out on the stream. Even though there is no door nobody can see in.

I have bathed in the stream. I plunged into a pool of peaty brown water but very clear and then soaped myself before I washed it off. It was hard to get my hair clean. I had to put my clothes on over my wet body. I have decided to shave every day because I think it is good for me. I like the clean feel even though nobody comes round.

My only friend seems to be a dog which comes down from the station house and seems to have adopted me. I have little to feed him on but he doesn't seem to mind. He is a great tall lurcher, a cross of retriever, collie and greyhound, I think, and has yellow eyes and a long, lolling head with red ears. He comes and lies by my fire. I whistle to him and he seems to understand.

I miss Gregory too and would like to tell him more things. Please remember me to him.

He signed it with his affection again.

The fire was very hot against him, burning almost like charcoal with grey logs of fallen broadleaf. He could see the flames through the big beetle grub holes in it. The dog was stretched out, not even twitching in its sleep. He could boil his big black kettle for tea now, slung by its round handle on a fireplace hook. His stomach was comfortable with bacon he had fried and a damper, a kind of scone he had made with flour and water twisted on a stick and baked in the ashes. Soon the manuka trunks would dry out and he could saw them up in the 'horse' he had nailed up from their straighter branches while the dead bark stuck to his hands. It was firm enough.

The pony cart stopped as he was at the race peering through at the redd, as he now thought of it. There was no change. The eggs shone on the rocks. There were two women in the trap. They looked at him intently as he walked out, the dog following him closely. He put his hand down and could feel its head by his left knee and scratched the hard cartilage around its ear. It leaned into him.

"That's our dog." The blonde woman who was holding the reins seemed to be accusing him. The other beside her was slightly heavy under her dark hair, with a detectable little moustache he did not like over her thin lips. "Yes. It's a very important dog," she said and seemed to nudge Mary, like a conspirator.

"Why's that?"

"It roams around at night and chases off the wild dogs that try to come in off the hill and get our calves and foals or the sheep in the yard for the killing."

"It's very important to us. But I think it comes and lies by your fire instead of being out," the other woman said.

"I can't help that. It just comes."

"You probably gave it food, that's why. We like to keep it thin so it will chase the wild dogs away."

"It can run very fast but you'll be making it lazy."

The dog nuzzled his knee. He had a sudden vision of the girl washing herself.

"Can we see the eggs?" the dark one said. "It took a long time to put in the ponds and hut and things."

Albion walked up to the cart while the pony shifted. It looked like the grey cob he had been promised. He held up his hand for the dark woman to get down. Close up she seemed a little older, about twenty.

"That's Denebola. My companion. Help me too, please." He did not like the way she seemed to think it her right to see the redd, as if she had to make proprietorship clear.

The dog sidled away from him, looking back at the women as if they were not friends. "Denebola — that's the name of a star. The sky's very bright out here at night."

The sun had risen over the roof of the race now and there was no reflection on the water. They looked and said nothing. Denebola took off a black glove and trailed a little finger in the water. "There's nothing much to see."

He felt disappointed in himself and the eggs, possessive of them and not at all wanting them to be shown.

"It will take about three weeks for them to hatch. Then you'll see the little fish with their yolk sacks. They're called alevin. They use up their yolks in twenty-one days. I'll keep them behind a screen and then I'll let them go in the pond."

"We'll come again," said Miss McIvor, and giggled. "Won't we, Denebola?"

"That would be interesting. More interesting than this."

Albion turned and looked down the ponds. He could hear a sad, down-falling lilting bird song in the bush, a grey warbler perhaps. At the corner of his eye he thought he saw something move against the bullrushes and tried to focus to see if it was really there.

"I think there's a bittern down there. I haven't heard it croaking yet but I suppose I'll have to scare it away from the little fish."

"The dog might help. His name's Tad," Denebola said.

"But don't be too kind to him." Miss McIvor was disapproving. "And make sure you turn him out at night time. There's lots of wild dogs out there. They hang around the sheep and all our shepherds have to carry guns to shoot them. They're very sly, though."

Is that what you are, Albion thought, desiring her as she straightened and walked back to the trap. Denebola smiled at him as if she understood.

"I'll make sure he's turned out, then. You don't mind giving me milk, do you? And could I come for some eggs? And in a week or two I'll need sheep livers to feed the fish on. I'll come for meat — is that all right?"

"Of course," she said. "I just thought I'd warn you about the dog." He put his hand under her round arm as she got back to the reins.

"He's a very useful dog," Denebola said while he handed her. She did not look at him. She looked at Mary.

"Oh, and some butter, too?"

"Mrs Barclay makes her own yeast in a big jar. She bakes bread. When you come for the milk again I'll show you where they kill the sheep." She slapped the reins on the cob.

"Thanks for showing us," Denebola called, looking back, kind, he thought, with her dark eyes. Then, the dog would stay with him, that was clear. There was something good between him and the dog whatever they said about the way he chased away the shaggy wild things that lived on the moor.

Denebola was a star name. It was bright towards the meridian from Ursa Major, to the right of the zodiacal constellation of Leo and just under Virgo. The quiet Tad was again beside him and he wondered at the fleetness and rage of his long teeth. White fog was coasting down the valley hills to the north, and in the south a boiling grey front seemed to be coming. The pond was still for the moment, and two Paradise duck, white headed and green over their bronze, were swimming on it.

DEEP STREAM
APRIL 28, 1868

> *Dear Charlotte,*
> *Rain is heavy on the roof and I am afraid that the stream will rise. It could easily flood across the flat where my pond is. Mary McIvor and her companion-maid Denebola came yesterday in a pony and trap and were rude to me about my dog. They said the dog was theirs and would roam around at night to chase away wild dogs that came after the stock. Tad is so gentle with me that I find that hard to believe but the women were quite polite, I suppose, and wanted to see the eggs. There wasn't much to show them yet. God that rain is heavy and the wind is in the bush up the flat. I wonder what the birds do in a storm. I've got in quite a store of wood so I will be all right in here.*

He broke off there for a moment because the rain sounded so heavy.

> *Today I went for milk and took a stock of flour for Mrs Barclay to bake into bread for me. She is a gaunt woman with staring pale*

blue eyes that seem to make her more grey and tall but she received me kindly. Miss McIvor then led me up to the woolshed where she said the cowman would kill a sheep.

He had seen, he remembered now, the disturbed and desperate look in the sheep's eye as the man, with heavy hands, took out the knife. She, like him, was no stranger to butchery, and as the blood sprayed forth he was again standing by his father, feeling the knife hilt in his right hand as he bent the sheep's head up with his left and tried to cut. The sheep squirmed under him and he could feel the knife slipping over the neck wool.

"Harder — hard and clean," his father said. "You've got to learn to put your weight into it. Otherwise you won't cut through the sinews, see? Use your shoulder."

Again he struck the blow and this time the head lolled. The eye looked up at him.

"Thrust it away quick," his father said. "Let it drain on the floor." Scraps of straw stuck to the eye. The beams of the barn bore down on him in the half-dark, lighted only by the open door. "Now haul it up to the hooks and stick its hind legs on, just at the ankles. Feel them?" The body hung twitching on the double hook and blood drained on his boots. "Now's the time you put a good cut in, down the belly so the guts will drop out." He learned to skin and how the knife point could sever the joints for the table. "Good boy. Wait till you see what your mother does with that."

He had barely been strong enough. He looked at Miss McIvor.

She seemed to be blushing, looking away. "That's what we do," she said. "You'll be wanting to come for the livers soon, to boil them and mince them, I suppose."

"We walked away from the shed and I said I'd only seen her father once, at the Society meeting. She said he was a doctor of laws and he advised with railways and steel in Scotland. I asked about her mother and she said that she had decided to stay in Edinburgh and not come to the new country. 'My Father said that there had to be one woman of the family here.' I was only fourteen but I had to come.

"He is a very dear father," she had said suddenly but he was walking close enough to think that she shivered. "He's such a tall man." The shadow over them was huge and black. A harrier circled over the kitchen garden looking about to stoop at yellow robins and waxeyes around the young fruit trees there. He wrote on.

The rain seems even harder now. It is noisy on the window. I will have to go out to look at the stream which I think might be rising by now. I am afraid for the eggs. This will be the first time that I wear the mackintosh cape you gave me and the sou' wester. I am afraid for what I will find. Remember me to the blue lion, dear Charlotte.

Outside the rain was silver in the lantern beam. The dog raised himself shivering from the fire and outside shook the water from his eyes. Water was running swiftly through the ditch from the stream into the egg race. He could just see, as he slipped on the mud, that it was oily and brown. It drew off silt from the sides of the ditch. Little avalanches of earth and shingle fell in. He grabbed a sack of coal which leaned against the hut, staggered with it until he could throw it into the ditch. The water dammed back and he shoveled earth and shingle around it, almost blind now that he had put the lantern down, his arms already aching, his ears ringing with the rasp. Rain clattered all over him and he blew the water from his mouth. In the lantern light again he could see that the flow had almost stopped yet there had to be enough to keep the eggs covered. He bent again and smoothed the ditch sides until he thought enough flowed around the coal. Now he could only wait and wonder if there was anything to pray to. A piece of driftwood lodged against the coal. There were still green leaves on it. The stream had torn it away. He watched a while but water was being driven under his mackintosh, seeping under his belt. He could feel it trickling on his thighs. The dog idly scratched at the ditch edge and he wanted to hit it with the shovel handle but growled it away instead. He raised his face and let the rain sting it. The stream was loud and water shot into his ears.

In the dripping morning he found that the eggs on their slabs were covered with a fine layer of brown silt. He wondered if they would be able to breathe.

At the station door, he still in his sou' wester but changed into his oilskin jacket, Miss McIvor smiled at him.

"The rain," he said, "I had to dam the ditch and now my eggs are all covered with silt. I have to get it off somehow. Can you help me? I have heard that all young ladies like to paint in water colours and I wonder if you have a brush, a fine camel hair brush would do, and I could clean off the silt very gently if you could lend such a brush to me."

"It's true that I paint with water colours but I don't think I'm very good at it. I do it to pass the time."

"So could you lend me one of your brushes — a very fine camel hair?"

"I probably have such a brush. I was sent a whole new package by my father in Wellington. He sent new paints. I have scarcely used them. But the eggs are so small. Wouldn't they be moved around? I will go and see what I have got."

When he put the brush down on his table he saw that there was a black blot of ink on his letter to Charlotte and he scribbled his apologies at the bottom. Then he lit the fire again and cooked himself a breakfast of fried bacon.

The stream roared through its boulders but the race was running clear again. She was right, he thought. It was hard not to move the eggs around with the brush as he cleaned them and he was afraid of bruising them on the schist. Puffs of silt floated away. After many hours his hand was white and wrinkled but the silt was gone, the eggs red again with their spot eyes gleaming. In a few days they would be hatching out.

He heard the creak of the pony cart wheels before it came. He was watching the eggs split, the tiny pale fish uncoiling from them, resting a moment and then beginning to swim facing the current. They were almost transparent. He could see the black lines of their bones in this extraordinary birth. Joy overwhelmed him and he bent to rub the dog's ears. It pressed against his groin.

"We've brought you a cheese," the voice called out. He handed them down from the cart. "It's just a cream cheese dripped in a bag."

"But I moulded it in muslin and cured it," Denebola said.

There were more alevin alive, darting in the water, when they went to look. More eggs split.

"It makes one feel strange," Mary said.

Denebola seemed to be peering very deeply into the water, a strand of hair falling down." I used to try and think about what made things," she said. "I decided for a long time that it must be the colour purple — or rather a bright violet blue. I decided that that was what I believed was making things."

Albion did not want to interupt her but she continued talking, as if to herself. "I saw that colour everywhere and it was making things all right. I could tell." She laughed. "Then I thought that if it was everywhere it couldn't be special to me. I had to think that I shared it. I had to think that I only took part in it. I had to understand that it was doing things that I could not control. I had to realise that it was putting limits on me." She took off her glove and trailed a finger in the water again. "And then, then Mary came along and asked me to help her. And I had to think there must be something else but the colour violet blue and I didn't know what it was. So I just had to let myself be and keep on trying to do things that were . . ." She seemed lost for words. "Well, 'helpful', I suppose. Yes. That's how it seemed to me then."

Albion found that he was wanting to say at the same time as Mary, "And then what happened?" but she said it first.

"Out here," Denebola said, "we go around in the pony trap and go up to Clarke's Junction for the mail when a waggon doesn't bring it by and we walk in the garden and sometimes I feel a kind of contentment and I still feel that colour all around me. And now look at all these little fish." She laughed and shook her fingers, and put her glove back on.

Albion kept watching from time to time throughout the day. Clouds moved away from the sun. He heard the bittern croaking brownly in the rushes. The late afternoon was cool and still with gold on the dark broadleaf trees up by the ditch he had dammed. On the meander meadow the grass was dark and short among patches of cushion weed, red where the shingle was at the surface. McIvor must have scattered grass seed on the better ground. Suddenly he could see that it was covered in places with tiny hearts-ease flowers that had opened after the rain and in spite of the autumn. He picked up one of the wild pansy shapes, a fiery red and yellow splash in a crown of bright violet blue. The bloomy petals were firm and proud among the leaves, another English plant that was already so casually growing here but precious to him in the lengthening shadows. He had wanted to ask her if she had first seen the colour, un-aided, in her head. Had it just come to her or had she 'seen' it. He would have to write to Charlotte about 'seeing' things. The Dunstan Road was a pale scrawl across the moors at his back. *Viola tricolour*, that was the botanical name of hearts-ease. He would never forget it now.

Always in the morning when he woke he would note the low sun coming. He chuckled at the slight delay when he put on his socks, before the warm hairiness tickled the soles of his feet. For a moment the hut would look harsh, bare and cold and he thought of the dog's wounded stare in the lamp light at the door when he was put out punctually every night. He took his slop bucket to the stream and, looking at the curling water, remembered how the soap foam from his pale body would fall, turn and flow down in spirals around the rocks, caught sometimes for a moment before it dissappeared. Always in the morning as he rinsed his bucket he would see sunlight on a white mark gleaming at him from the western hill, beyond the water. Then one morning he put the bucket on the bank and slopped across the ford, mindless of wet boots and trouser legs. He climbed up through the tussock, unable to grip on it and sometimes nearly tripping as he stood on one fold of leaves and put his other foot through the hole, wrenching his ankle. Up the hill, as if his whole being was caught in a shadow of the golden light that seemed just there, he came to a wooden slab set in the ground over an old hump of earth. On it was painted carefully in woolshed tar:

In memory of

James Andrew Barclay
May 3, 1857 – April 16 1862
God rest his soul
Taken so early

He had heard tales of a brother, a baby died of small pox before he was born, his mother and father sweating to make him, a replacement, that's all he was while corn crakes stalked in the water meadow below his cottage and hares played. He learned to skate there when it was frozen, even in the spring when the early hawthorn hung white over the ice and its thorns were like blades. This boy was buried with his feet to the east, his head to the setting sun, going where he had voyaged before.

A letter came again from Charlotte while he waited the three weeks it would take the alevin to use up their yolk sacs and he could lift the mesh that kept them from pouring into the pond in which they would grow.

LANCASTER HOUSE
MAY 8, 1868

> *I went down to the restaurant again and Elegant Cheng met me as usual. He had a poem for me which I have tried to remember for you. It went something like, 'I wonder what year this is in the palaces of heaven. I must ride the wind and return to the moon. The moon should not have anything against me. The moon has dark and light which never ends. I just wish we could live a long time.' I haven't remembered very well, I think, but that's the gist of it that I seemed to get. 'Very old poetry,' he said and smiled at me. Tell me about all the things in your world. The bath got blocked and I had*

to get a plumber man up to clear it. Plumbers are quite new here because we have not had the water before and the gas has not been brought up here yet.

He remembered his father peeling an orange, how the pith stuck to his dirty fingers and his horned nails, an orange very rare up there and come all the way from warmer islands. His father licked up the falling juice and the pieces were wet on his mouth. The winter air stung with orange spray from the broken skin. Soon he would have to feed the salmon fry which would weigh less than an ounce. Every ten days they would double their size. In the spring they would be between an ounce and five if they took the food well and were not caught. He had seen an eel in the stream and if it got into the pond it would eat the fry.

"I'm going up the pasture. I could show you if you like," Barclay said one day at his door. They splashed across the stream and began to climb. "That's where our son's put in the ground. Some miners came by in a waggon. We let them stop and they had the scarlet fever with them. It wasn't long before our boy was sick. We couldn't bear to take him all the way down to the cemetery so we put him up here. Look, there's not many flowers out at this time of year but this here's a harebell." He combed away the tussock and Albion could see a pale blue flower on a reed stem. He showed him grasses sheep could eat under the tussock and a tiny geranium. Lower down, among the trees, he put his fingers gently under bunches of berries and seed cases.

"I don't burn. Some of the runholders burn. They says the grass comes away better after it but you can never tell what the fire will do and I don't want to have to be out with the plough to make a fire break round the house. I do it my way, whatever Dr McIvor says, and we get a good clip off it. An old Maori came and showed me these tree things. He was shepherding for a while and he told me with the Maori names but I've forgotten. You should see it in spring, though."

Albion touched the seed pods of a broom tree and felt the harsh leaves of rangiora, wineberry, whitey wood, matipo and lemon wood, five finger, ribbon wood, lance wood and ngaio, the little spears of mountain totara. He felt moss and his hands were torn with matagouri. Wild Spaniard spiked through his trousers. He pushed grass trees aside. He tasted the pink and white snow berries and they were faintly sweet, like old bread.

"Now look at that — never seen the like. It must've got confused." Barclay pointed to the red bell flowers hanging from an old fuchsia and rubbed the papery copper skin off its bark.

"That's mighty early for a flower. And look underneath where I rub. It's bright green. Even the sap's got it wrong." He kicked away a rock with his heavy boot. "When we put the cutting in from the stream for water for that pond he got all carried away. Said we could bring in a golden kind of frog from Australia. There were none here but you can hear them calling sometimes already. And then he brought a pair of white-faced herons and when he said he could use the ponds for the salmon I wondered about that because the birds would eat them, wouldn't they. And they've grown and taken to nesting in the pine trees that have come away around the house, all sticks and very untidy. There's enough with our own blue heron, I think, and we see the white one in the winter some times. Like an old ghost, standing there." They passed through bracken fern up to their thighs, wet with dew in the shade.

Albion went to the cowman for butchered liver and carried it dripping to the stream. As he washed away the blood and membranes that stuck he felt a soft nibbling at his finger and saw a little eel come with the taste. He reared up like a horse and then wondered why he was so frightened. The eel vanished.

He began to boil the liver in a big black pot over his fire. The cooked pieces were dry once they were cool and the smell had stopped but they clogged in the knife plates of his mincer and he had to strive, putting the mess through again and again to get it fine enough to throw in the pond. When the meal landed on the water there were tiny splashes as the fry immediately began to feed. In a far corner a grebe and a dabchick floated. He saw the white flash of a swamp hen's rump and looked for a frog. That night he slept deeply after he put the dog out and wondered what he would write to Charlotte. He would take sheets from the blotter in his letter case, gather plants and press them dry in front of his fire so that she would understand.

Dear Charlotte,
I have seen more of the property. There was fire smoke on the horizon to the West but the wind is blowing it away. I have made the livers into a kind of powder which I throw out beyond the rushes and the fish seem to seethe over it so I presume they are learning to eat. Thank you for the poem. I need books. There won't be many book shops there yet but can you try in the town. I would relish having some Carlyle and Browning and Tennyson, some Brontes — my village isn't far from where they come from and I went to the same sort of school — and Eliot and Disraeli but I'll have to leave it up to you to see what you can do. On the coach would do and they will drop them off. . . .

Dear Dan,
I hope that it is not a trouble to you but I will need some more stores soon. I hunger for onions and pumpkin and swede. Even a cabbage would keep for a while, I think. I need something to put in my mutton stew or have with the roast I do in my camp oven. Are there some pickles there? I think of beets and walnuts and those with hot

mustard. I love tomato pickle very much but I doubt that is available. In any case, do you mind if I give you a list. I need more flour and potatoes. Mrs Barclay at the station bakes bread for me but I'm at the bottom of the flour bag. Tea I will soon be short of, and salt. Lamp oil and candles. I have made a list if that is all right . . . .

When it began to snow they sent the cowman. "Not lying yet," he said at the door. "But from the look of it it won't be long." Albion could see flakes on his eyelashes. He handed up a folded card.

SIX

MISS MARY McIVOR and MISS DENEBOLA ROBERTS request the pleasure of the company of MR ALBION DUFFY at tea today if the snow does not inconvenience him.

The strong black shag moved fast across his sight from right to left over the pond. He stood hesitant at half past three, the snow thicker now on his woolly hat and the long lapels of his oilskin jacket. The muffler was warm but he felt for a moment as muscled and stringy as the bird which seemed to reach like a goose and swept the air with a noise. It circled as if looking to land with its huge wings stretched out. He wondered if he had time to get his gun, the double-barreled piece in the corner of his hut, the draped powder flask and leather bag of percussion caps, cotton wads and the pouch of shot. As he blinked the snow away he watched the shag head off to the west, a deadly dragon come suddenly to haunt him with its promise of diving and fishing, the yellow beak hooked down on top and stretched out. His fingers itched in his mittens but he walked on with the snow already icing his insteps, making his ankles feel higher.

"You are fortunate," Miss McIvor said smiling in the parlour. "Mr Barclay found a bees' nest with honey in the bush the other day."

He poured the syrupy stuff over his pikelets with clotted butter from a brown bottle, had to lick his fingers and wipe them on the linen napkin. "I went up and saw the grave. I had not known that there was a child. So long ago."

"There is not much cure for the fever."

"I suppose Dr Lister's discovery of microbes in the air and the way they cause disease will help."

"To put a poultice on a sore throat you make a pulp of a roasted apple. You mix it with an ounce of tobacco and wet it with spirits of wine. Then you spread it on a linen rag and bind it to the throat," Denebola said.

"You ought to know — you can cure the hard cough with a linen rag soaked in butter and sprinkled with yellow Scotch snuff. You can get grease from a goose and pour that down the throat, too."

"Even this new country has its cures. You can cut off some pieces of flax near the ground to get at the gummy part and then you boil it in water. It's dark when it is strained. I'm told that it's good for pain in the joints and it's a strong laxative."

"Pooh," said Miss McIvor. "Let's play dominoes."

"Oh, don't be prudish, Mary. You can clean your skin and your kidneys with parsley tea. Did you know that?"

Mary put a woollen bag of dominoes on the table. "Do you want to play?"

"I will be happy to watch," said Denebola. "In a moment I will go and get a pot and some spices and some wine and put it on the fire to mull. You can cut people open now and take bits out of their innards and they won't feel a thing — they'll be asleep after you make them breathe chloroform." She put a log on the fire.

Albion turned over a domino. It was polished wood with the dots counter-sunk in each end so that they held shadows. Mary lit the lamps. Outside snow drifted in spirals from a black sky. He could see it lying on a bunch of orange rowan berries. Rowan stakes were said to ward off witches and the spirits of the dead like the strange spiral marking carved in ancient stones, and it was said in the vision of Ezekiel that God showed Himself 'out of the whirlwind'.

"Shall we play Muggins?" Miss McIvor said, turning the dominoes over so that only their blank faces showed. "You take seven and the rest are the pool."

"How do you play? Can you build on doubles in your game? No, of course you can't. Muggins is trying to make all your building in multiples of five, isn't it."

"Doubles are placed crosswise and no building," she said. "If you can not play you must draw from the pool. I win if I get to sixty-one first."

Albion found that he struggled sometimes to work out the numbers quickly. He pondered a long time and seemed to draw from the pool often. He knew he was losing when Denebola came back with a pot to place on the fire, china cups and a ladle. The dominoes clacked down. Every one of the twenty-eight was baleful.

"They say the domino was a kind of fancy dress and you had a mask on a stick to cover your eyes," he said to gain time. "I heard the idea came from a notion of the dark Lord — the Prince of Darkness."

Mary shivered — in a theatrical way, he thought. "Ssssh. Don't spoil it for me."

Denebola, without a word, ladled the cups and served them

on each side. "It's got real honey and cloves and nutmeg and cinnamon sticks," she said.

"Would you prefer to play Matador?" Mary said. She counted her win. "It's all built on sevens — you take seven pieces and you have to build on the line to make seven or you can play a Matador which is a piece that adds up to seven on its own. And when you pass you don't have to take one from the pool. It's more of a gamble, I think."

Heartened by the wine, Albion agreed. "I'm a bad gambler," he said. "But I will try it." He lost again as they sipped their wine and looked at each other. It was the first time that she looked him full in the face. Her nipples dripping water.

"Many people have thought that dominoes could be put together in a different way," said Denebola. "You could join them up in threes, for instance, so that each person had to play three at once and match up the spots."

"That sounds complicated."

"Well, it's like the old problem of how you double the size of a cube — you can't just double the base sides because the result would be a cube that was four times as big."

"I didn't know that women looked for answers like that."

"We are definitely not supposed to," Mary said.

"But when I was at school I took to all that. The answer about the cube is that you have to take the cube root of the volume first and proceed from there."

"I could never understand it properly," Albion said, and held out his cup to her. "You seem to be well versed in mathematics."

"Oh, that is just one of her skills. What could you expect from someone who is named after a star? Soon we are to go to Dunedin for a ball. Won't that be amusing, Denebola? You have lost again, Mr Duffy, I think."

"Never mind. I am fortunate to have played with you and

learned. I was thinking of a black shag. I saw one fly over the pond as I came. I wanted to shoot it in case it went fishing for my smolt."

"Oh please, Mr Duffy, and please be careful with your gun and please don't shoot the white-faced heron that my father brought over for the pond."

"But the fish! What if the herons start . . . ?" He did not finish because she was gathering up the dominoes.

"Scarecrows," he thought, as he crunched back through the snow which was now four inches thick on the ground. "I can cut tussock for their bodies and heads, tied up in shapes I can put on manuka sticks, and there are probably old hats and jackets left behind in the shearers' lodgings by the woolshed. One on each side of the pond." The native birds would notice them but were the white-faced herons too used to man?

He put the dog out that night. At first it ran around curious and biting at the snow, than turned to him, humiliated and beginning to shiver, but it would have to keep warm by running and wild dogs were sure to creep closer to the homestead in the frozen night. But sunbeams spread from his window in the morning. Snow slid from the roof and thumped on the ground outside as he pulled the blankets up. Then a strange scratching began on the roof and he forced himself up to open the door. A pair of kaka parrots flew away with a whistling noise so he lit his fire, kneeling for the flames to heat his chest. Breasts dripping water. Her blondeness over the table, the rich taste of hot wine. If the thaw continued, the road to the Junction might clear. Stuffed cabbage, Denebola had said. If he got a cabbage he could peel back the leaves, put in mutton he could mince when he finished the liver, and flour and pickle, and tie it up again in a shape and boil it if Dan remembered.

Dear Albion,

Your letters tell me so much. I have found some books for you and Dan has made up your stores. This will go on the passenger and mail coach which will be sooner to get to you. They want to have a high school and a university here. I think that is wonderful for such a small place. We are all very busy. Mavis and Dolly send their best wishes. Henry is going with his waggon as far as Palmerston on the new road north past Blueskin Bay over those awful hills. There are rumours of good steaming coal to be found beyond the Shag River near Palmerston and that will help the railway plans as well as making plenty of work for Henry. John is busy on the railway line to Fairfield where they are making bricks we need for all the new buildings in the town.

My music teacher, Miss Yates, is proving very good. I am learning scales. She says she will get me to play Bach who wrote pieces for beginners on the harpsichord. She even showed me the original notes they used to play on the ancient Pipes of Pan. She says that they are in order the notes F, G, C and E flat. I wonder how she knows but I play them and they sound good.

My big news is that I am going to a ball. It is the Volunteers Ball and Dan is taking me in his uniform with his sword. It is to be in the banqueting hall of the Provincial Council and will be very grand because they have gas lights on the walls now as well as crystal chandeliers. All the officers will be there, he says, but he says he does not know much about dancing. I will have to teach him. Thora has patterned a ball dress for me and Yvonne is making it in fine oyster-coloured silk which suits me. I will have red shoes and gloves, my favourite colour. I wonder when you will do my Tarot again. Whatever it is, it seems to have something of the truth in it, doesn't it?

She had not written about Gregory or the monkey in her letter and he found himself feeling diminished without knowing why, a kind of moroseness. Perhaps she had her reasons and that was her business but could she be hiding something? She was so frank that he did not think that this was likely but his feelings continued.

Dear Mr Henty,
I would like to be able to report to you that all is going well here but I am afraid I am not able to at the moment. Everything should be proceeding with peace and calm. The eggs have hatched in good time and I released the fry into the pond when they grew large enough. My accommodation here is very satisfactory and I am receiving books and stores from friends in Dunedin but I have had a sore stomach of late and I am mystified as to the cause of it. I am eating well but my spirits are low.

I have built scarecrows to frighten birds away from the pond and put one on either side of it, suitably lifelike, but the other morning I came out and saw a black shag that has been flying about, perched on the head of the farther one, its wings spread out to dry, like a gaunt spectre after its dive. I had to shoot it and it went down in fine style, flapping at the far side of the pond, among the bulrushes, or raupo as I believe it is called. If you will forgive my saying so I think it was a fair shot at more than 40 yards and there was little damage to my 'crow.

But then I found to my horror that a young eel was escaping from its craw, wriggling away to the water and I decided, after some careful examination, that the pond is infested with eels. They have come in down the race from the stream. I am afraid that I am quite unable to understand how Dr McIvor, who is a member of our Society committee, could have allowed this to happen and built the pond so, when he arranged to have it used to hatch salmon eggs. Was this the act of a man informed about natural life? I am further very disturbed to find that Dr McIvor has brought in white-faced heron from Australia and proceeded to acclimatise them even though they are known to prey on little fish.

In spite of my infirmity I have been hard at work trying to make eel traps and can only do it in an old Maori way I have been told about, out of flax. With these I hope to rid the pond of eels that, even as I write, are eating my fish and they are small in number in any case. My urgent request to you is that you should send up to me immediately a quantity of close iron mesh that I can put in the inlet water and prevent further infestation from the stream.

I cannot emphasise too strongly the urgency of this request. The mail coach gets to Clarke's Junction from Dunedin in a few hours and I believe they would carry such an urgent parcel.

Your obedient servant etc.,

Albion found that his pain was not eased even by this letter, or the books which Charlotte sent, or the stores from Dan.

While he raged inside he made eel traps and sank them with stones in various parts of the ponds. He heard the pony trap rattle away in the distance and guessed that it was carrying the two women towards the ball. It was even worse that Charlotte was going to it in her long gloves, to the heady music, the laughter and the gas light.

He took his gun and fired at the bittern, glad that he missed and then full of loathing for himself for trying. It seemed that the time would never pass. He sweated at night and could not find refuge, even in the doorless privy by the stream. When he lifted his eel traps he poured out the wriggling catch and, on the grass, viciously beheaded the eels with his axe. Their bodies kept on wriggling among the guts. After a few days he felt calmer. The ball must be long over with its heat and noise, and no more eels came to the bait of sheep's heads he sank. He felt exhausted and even the dog seemed to slink around him instead of standing tall with a twitching nose. He saw Mr Barclay driving the pony trap into the station yard with the two women.

"I had a bad time with eels while you were away," he told them bitterly when he went to ask for eggs. A heavy woollen shawl covered her bosom. "But I shot the black shag."

He tried to keep a note of triumph from his voice and they told him they had been asked to dance every dance at the ball which was very grand and well lit with a fine supper and even champagne. Everything was there to spark the imagination, Denebola said, looking sharply at him. His fingers were still stiff from fashioning flax strips and raupo fibres into eel traps with narrow mouths.

Dear Mr Duffy,
You should by now have taken delivery of some pieces of metal mesh that I hope will suffice to help out with your eel problem.

Indeed they had. He had cursed and sweated cutting manuka posts to shape, picking and shovelling at the intake ditch, piling in the posts and burying the edge of the nailed mesh in the ditch bottom. He hoped that the bag of coal had stopped a further infestation of eels from the stream.

I hope that you are feeling well again. I am afraid that I felt some consternation at your remarks re. Dr McIvor. You are at the hatchery because Dr McIvor has been kind and far-sighted enough to build the pond and make it available to the Society of which he is an influential and valued member, having done much in the cause of the acclimatisation of wild life which is the Society's aim. Dr McIvor's generosity has been gratefully received with great esteem rendered to him by the Society. I do not think that it is proper that you should question that generosity, whatever your emotions should be about the rearing of Atlantic salmon whose eggs were brought across the sea by the Society at great expense, in the circumstances in which you find yourself.

*Dear Albion,
Just a note to go with the books. We all hope that you enjoy them and that they will help you in your vigil — is that the right word? Love. Charlotte.*

*Dear Albion,
I followed your list carefully and hope that you receive all the goods you need in fair condition, as I sent them. I took the liberty of sneaking in a bottle of kirsch for you which I hope you might find to warm you. When I go to the top of the hill up in Roslyn I look out over the hills and the snow seems to be well down and has been for a good time now. Cheers. You may depend upon me for anything you need. All well here. Dan.*

With this mail Albion was both gratified and concerned that the goodwill of the Society seemed to have been threatened. He looked at the cut glass bottle of kirsch, the brandy made from cherry juice in Europe so far away, and decided that he might take a nip. It might warm him like the fire which must be stoked. The snow was thick now, outside his hut and ice crackled in the bulrushes when he went to throw the liver meal to his fish.

"It's time we saw where you lived," they said at his door one afternoon when frost still made the snow crusty. "So we put on our cloaks and stout boots and our mufflers and had to come."

"I am sure that there is a recipe for pancakes made with snow,"

Denebola said when they had sat down together on his bed. He sat at his chair trying to look welcoming, looking at Mary erect on the bed, at the colour in her face, wondering if it was for him or if it was the cold. "It has currants in it and I seem to remember that the snow makes for a very light batter in the pan. They are said to be crisp and delicious."

"I have only molasses to sweeten them. But if you get the snow I will make them for you. I've got the currants and plenty of flour now, and your good eggs."

He gave her a cup to scoop snow up at the door, and fried the cakes in his pan. They had to lick their fingers, wipe them on his dish cloth and then on their skirts, laughing at the mess.

"You seem to be very cosy here," Mary said, opening her eyes wide at him. "Does the dog always come to your fire?"

"I put him out every night and he has a hurt look. But that is what you asked me to do."

"Obviously he has grown to love you."

"I can only offer you a little kirsch and only in my tin pannikins or there's an old china cup I found here. It might warm you for your walk."

They looked at each other and gasped as they sipped but they said it was better than champagne. He sipped from an old egg cup and felt better.

"It is strange how dogs love people."

"I have often wondered what makes people," Denebola said.

"Fish," said Albion. "They have back bones like we do."

"But fish — how could people have come from them?"

Albion hesitated but suddenly felt that he should dare. "If you look in a microscope, at the seeds that a man produces, you see that they all have heads and little threshing tails. They are swimming like fish."

"But I thought that if you saw those seeds you could see tiny men in them."

"That's a very old idea. That's what they thought more than a hundred and fifty years ago after the microscope was invented."

"So how could people love them?" Denebola said. "Are they like dogs then? Do fish fall in love?"

"The first thing the fish eggs get is eyes. And they say that beauty is in the eye of the beholder."

"But the feeling. Where do feelings come from?" Mary was asking him at last.

"Dogs seem to have loyalty and devotion," Albion said. "And they have a very keen sense of smell, and of hearing."

"And we have to keep Tad so that he will fight and devour," Denebola said. "Is that part of it too?"

'I think that there is some preparation it it — in love or war or making us ready for any vast emotion. There is a difference between heredity and inheritance. It's like a natural selection of species. It's one of the great limit laws of biology. The characteristics one has or displays are perhaps not inherited but nevertheless they go to make up our heredity as a human being — or a dog, for that matter."

Mary was looking down, picking with the fingers of both hands at a dark thread in her shawl. He wanted to sit beside her and feel her shoulder against him. The skin on his back prickled, his chest wanted to be against her blouse.

"My father's coming soon," she said. "He wrote to say that he would spend a few days here before they muster for the shearing."

"I hope that he will like me," Albion said and understood what he was being tempted to ask, there and then, in his hut, with Denebola there and she was precise and full of logical questions he could not answer and looked at him, confusingly, as if she knew, as if she wondered why her intellect was not a more powerful attraction.

"Love," Albion said, immediately overwhelmed, "is a kind of marshalling of all the forces that make you an animal, as if all the good feelings that your body can give you are suddenly turned on. That's it."

He gave them another drink of kirsch before they left, frightened that the effects of the first would not be sufficient to carry them home through the waning dusk. There were his books and everything the women he had asked for could write for him about love and jealousy. It was a pity that they had not considered jealousy in their talk.

The dog would now sit when asked or shown a raised right index finger. He would lie with a command or the flat of a right hand, run out with a hand swinging forward while walking at heel, and stop at a shout or at the flat of a hand raised to him. He would keep going out or come in, whichever way he was gestured. Albion had taught him to jump a log or fetch a wound raupo ball, to stay in one spot while Albion hid himself and then come and find him at a whistle. He came when he was called, without fail and with no hesitation.

I am sure the monkey misses you.

Charlotte wrote in the spring.

> *I think he misses you more than he missed Grigori and his ship. He was very lively then at first and ran about lifting things and loking under them. Gregory keeps asking when you will be coming back. He is full of questions like 'How long do salmon live?' and 'Are horses as good as dogs to have? I want a dog.' You have not written for a long time except to thank me for the books. Are you all right?*
>
> *I have tried the mud! Yes, I've put it on my face. I fell in a panic*

because I thought I was a little dry but Logan said that the mud is made of the dead bodies of spirogyra which he said are little green spirally plants that grow in lakes and drop to the bottom when they are killed by ice. He said they were full of goodness so I took the mud and mixed it with some water as it was too dry. It made a kind of paste which I smeared into a mask on my face, being careful of my eyes. I left it on for a few hours and it went dry quite quickly. I could not smile and could hardly talk. Mavis and Dolly laughed at me. In the end I found that I could just peel it off and it did not stick but it left my face feeling lovely and fresh. I wondered what it would be like with a few drops of rose oil in it. It was quite a good idea, I think, and I will put it on again. Good old Logan. I must have looked a fright when I had it on but I could feel the good that it was doing. And then I wondered, if it feels good and helps me then what about other women? Logan left me maps and told me the signs about where you could find it in the mountains.

"My daughter seems very taken with you," said Dr McIvor a few days after Barclay had brought him down the hill in a spring cart that was painted new and used for the first time. "Denebola is enthusiastic in her praises, too. I value that young woman. She is a good companion in this lonely place that I have tried to make rich." He did not have a Scottish accent. "I would like you to come with me when we go out to look at the sheep before the muster."

He rode a big roan hack that made him seem even more tall, naked eyes under a wide black hat the wind kept bending. He would put his hand to it and Albion felt himself trying not to flinch on his grey cob. There was a light mist and his nose threatened to drip. All he could see was the tussock pressed silver as they began to move ahead. Sheep were all about them, their heavy fleeces wiry and close, the horned rams clubbed in groups, turned to them, aggressive.

"We'll go out towards the edge of the run. I want to make sure that the neighbour's fire has not encroached on me," he said, wheeling down a hollow in which fog rose. Nipples with water dripping. Dew? Dish water? A certain deadly ash-coloured wax? The world had become plain to him. His rough trousers ground on his thighs. "We need ten men here to fetch all these sheep in. Sometimes I wonder how they do it and I have to get the shearers here all at once. It's quite a plan. And then the women need to be taken care of with all those roughnecks about."

"You must be very busy — with Parliament and such a big property to run."

"I try to take care of things but I know that I am not always successful. I would happily have somebody else to help." His voice was softer now, falling away in the mist as he heeled his horse. "The women, that is what concerns me. By the way, thank you for having them to tea."

Those memories rose in him, her sitting on his bed. If he asked, this man could be his father-in-law. He could possess the grass as far as he could see.

"She is very precious to me, you know." He reined in on a knoll, his hands heavy, with hairs on the fingers caught with mist. Beside him Albion felt his youth though he was not so much younger. The girl was only seventeen. What would happen? He felt, when Dr McIvor turned round at him with a blank face, that he had been found out, as if he would soon be accused of something — his flickering pictures of her, some implied impropriety. His lust? He shuddered at it. The idea, the implication, whatever it was, was false. What if he did have yearnings? They were private. That was the essential thing. They were private.

"You find my daughter winsome," he said, as a statement. It

was like wrestling, with a wound that kept opening.

"She is a very attractive young lady."

"And you are all alone down there at the pond."

"I try to keep in touch with my friends."

"What friends? Is it not true that you have come out here looking for someone? All men do, I think."

The fog seemed thicker now. He's trying to bully me — that age-old persecution of boys by boys, he thought, but said only, "I have my work to do. I have to be content with that in the meantime."

He wheeled his horse. "There's not much point looking in this fog. I think we should go back. We can come out tomorrow after the sheep. You'll take dinner with us." He began to canter, as if sure of his way.

"I will have to go exploring," Albion said when he caught up and they began to walk towards the station buildings. "I would like to see where the stream comes out in the river gorge. I'll have to be away for a day or two. Getting there." All he got was a long stare.

"Have you any money?" Dr McIvor suddenly asked. "I suppose not. Pity. It would be a help."

Albion felt filled with resentment. He was being asked to marry her. He was considered a successful transplant across the Tropics, like one of the salmon eggs. Very well. It was logical that he would try to be so. There *must* be a logic in marriage. Surely that was logical even though it left many questions unanswered and carried the risk of needs unsatisfied as the new life grew. Might not misery be the result? He would have to take his chance.

He decided to refuse to say how much money he had. He had started with more than two thousand pounds from his inheritance. That was all, and his prospects looked less certain in spite of the invitation to partnership.

There was roast mutton. He looked at Mary across the table and a tide was in her eyes. "Did you go far with Dr McIvor?" she asked. "You came early. The weather is not good."

"I would be glad to go further some day," he said and thought that that was gallant of him. Spring. It was time to uncover his tarragon root and put it in the ground. There was a space by his door. He would level it and work in fowl manure. It was sheltered. He could water it. He would make little furrows, sow and cover the herb seeds from his packets. He would walk in the meadow and pick some heart's-ease which was blooming again. He would put it on his table in a little green bottle he had found. He thanked them for the meal. Denebola walked him out through the kitchen. "You are very welcome," she said, and then with a fine look he could not understand, she said, "God helps those who help themselves. Isn't that what they say?" and shut the door.

He found that Charlotte had sent him a cutting, wrapped in earth and sacking, of a climbing rose, a clump of carnations and some roots of iris. He noticed that the bittern had a frog in it beak, the legs pumping like trapped malicious gryphon wings as it was swallowed, bulging down the mottled neck. He took up his gun, his pouch of cotton wads, and began to polish the walnut stock with a little bacon grease from his pan. There were a couple of rust specks on the steel barrels so he dipped the wad in stream sand at his door and rubbed them away. He sighted and swung the gun, imagining flight from him. The dog leaped to its feet, wagging and eager. He taught himself to feel power again and wondered what it was for. Fog settled around his window. Something began to drip in his fireplace with a slight hiss. He rubbed more bacon grease into the leather of his boots.

He turned the flour bag he had emptied inside out and shook it, and found a length of small sisal stuff to tie it for a kitbag. He checked his powder and shot, found bags for oatmeal, salt, sugar, tea, and cut a piece of bacon. He put out a shirt and a pair of socks. He rolled his greatcoat and rolled it up with his cape. He would be ready to leave.

SEVEN

The billy, where he had tied it to his kit, banged against his back. The lid fell off and he stowed it instead. A band of pied stilts had come and was wading at the east end of the pond where it was more shallow. They flew when they saw him, piping loudly as if in farewell. He worried about the dog because it followed him and it would not be there that night. Never mind. He would keep to the right bank of the stream wherever he could.

His boots slid on the tussock. The gun grew heavy on his shoulder and he carried it at the trail, making sure that the dog did not scout too far ahead of him. He clambered over rocks and stood on bluffs, looking down into coppery pools that grew green at the deep centre. When dusk came he found a way down to the water's edge to look for firewood. A long weta floated by him upside down, its feelers and legs in a tangle. He shot a duck and found soft clay in the bank to wrap it in for baking as gypsies would do with hedgehogs. He carted the bird and the wood up the bank again to a small tussock flat above the fog that might gather over the stream. At dark he stood in wonder at the Milky Way that was clear and so bright above him that it hurt his eyes. They seemed to spark when he looked away. Then, low on the horizon, he could see Scorpio with Lupus, the wolf, ahead of it. Scorpio. Charlotte with mud on her face. He laughed. Scorpio was beginning to be bright and the big red star, Antares, under its centre hung like a pendant. Then he looked at Denebola above him, brighter yet.

When he had peeled clay and feathers from the duck he ate it, and threw the carcass and the shrivelled gut to the dog. He pulled his woolly hat down, wrapped his greatcoat tightly around him and lay down by the ashes. The dog, who had sat watching on the other side, came around to him, lay down beside him, licked his face and sighed heavily.

He woke in the dawn with a great trunking in his groin, his toes and fingers like spring blossom, dripping with nectar. The dog was away. He had dreamed. The pond was empty, a flat expanse of brown mud with baby eels still wriggling in it. A spoonbill waddled towards him, all white with its long black beak with a disk on the end, blown over the Tasman Sea from Australia by westerly winds. Its head bowed from side to side as it walked, picking up little fish and swallowing them, this side and that side without a sound as water trickled away. It had on a torn white blouse, came up and leaned over him with small hard breasts with nipples like walnut kernels that pressed into him. Its long dark hair was blonde at the roots. He shook himself and opened his eyes again. Standing, he emptied his bladder on the ashes — little grey clouds came up — and pushed gas from his bowel hoping that he would feel light and free but he did not.

He threw the cold tea from his billy and wiped it with tussock, then poured in some oatmeal and went to the stream for water. The bank grass was nibbled close and there were sheep droppings, some still shining. The sheep hurried away with long-tailed lambs, their feet leaving spoor in opposing half-moons where the ground was soft. They rattled in the rocks above him. He placed the billy on the edge. As he bent his shirt rubbed against his nipples. He felt it in his head. He swelled again like a tree to the sun and looked around in case there was anybody to see him. When he withdrew from her, his seed spilled and clotted on the grass and he came to himself thinking of Charlotte but his mouth had been on something wet and lightly haired, buttocks had pressed against him and round arms tangled him. The insides of his legs felt washed. He was afraid to move.

In the silence he found himself thinking, after a time, of marriage, then of Mary. He felt a great yearning for the land which she could bring within his grasp. There was no doubt that she could bring him children. He could found a dynasty! The thought excited him. He could give the sheep station a name which he chose himself. She would be gentle and loving and would take care of everything he hankered after. She would respect him. She would learn to follow the way he thought. They would come to believe in the same things. They would think, together, that there was nothing more important than their possession of the land and all it brought to them.

Up the hill he stared at the ashes of his fire. He wanted to heap the ashes on his head and rub them in to make cleansing soap with his body oils in penance. He made a fresh fire, ate porridge, calling the dog to him while cleaned his billy with stream gravel. He made tea. He was light. He remembered for a moment how he had lain on the grass unbuttoned, how colours had begun to swim in his head, at first climbing red, bands of yellow and green then finally suffusing shapes of purple in shimmers that wavered in his brain like slow silky flames in a black curtain edge in a wind that rose up his spine. He packed his camp and picked up his gun, feeling the straps of his swag bite lean on his shoulders.

For some reason the dog kept close to him as he sidled east to go round a gully with rocks that barred his way to the stream. He was slow as he stepped around the final corner, close to a kiln on his left. He fell back quickly. There was a sheep on the far side of the gully, its pink paunch showing and fleece torn back from its bloody thighs. A bitch was eating at it, with four pups. A tall dog stood to the side watching, with tight ears. Albion pressed Tad's haunches to their track and held up the flat of his hand. The air swirled and blew at them. 'I must do everything slowly,' he thought as he loaded heavy shot, drew back the hammers and placed priming caps. Was the hammer click too loud? He watched the end of the gun barrel as he lifted it clear to his shoulder, pulling it firm as he moved out. He shot the bitch dead and swung the choked barrel to the dog which stood at the shot. It somersaulted high in the air as the lead hit it and fell still.

Tad raced away in a huge lope across the gully. He ran after the pups, one by one, biting them once across the spine. They crawled about with broken backs, pulling themselves on their front legs. They screamed while Albion re-loaded with bird shot but as he ran over the tussock he felt for his knife. That would be quicker than shot. Then his hands knotted. He stood for a moment among the puppies.

Tad seemed to think he had done his best. His tongue hung out. Albion pulled the four necks, aware that he was looked at with hate. Milky teeth snapped at him. He flung the bodies away and felt sweat run on his back. The screaming stopped. He saw that the wild dog was still alive. He lifted its head with the gun muzzle in its mouth. It bit hard on the steel so that he felt it twist. He pulled the front trigger. The dog had looked directly at him, blazing with courage, daring him, and he would not forget.

He cut off the six tails. Perhaps Dr McIvor would like to see them. It is absurd, he thought. I want to put these bodies in a grave. He dragged them into a pile and went to see if he could break off pieces of schist to cover them. He could not so he had to walk on.

The country was steeper now and he knew that he must be close to the stream confluence. In the end there seemed no way but to go down into the cool bed of it. There was high, shadowy bush there and he stumbled over rocks and logs covered with moss and lichen until he came on a clearer space. In the middle of it stood the spiralled trunk of an old dead tree with hanging vines and a shower of white orchids like stars hanging. Then, along a still reach of water, he passed through a grove of pepper trees that were scarlet as if drawing their colour from the earth. He picked a leaf and it tingled in his mouth in the silence which had fallen as he walked around the dead tree. He had to push through the thickening pepper grove to climb down a small fall with ferns and liverworts until he was suddenly on a flat with widely spaced black beech trees. A robin came and squeaked at him with its bright yellow breast on a falling branch. A flock of green waxeyes fled ahead of him. A tiny rifleman passed quickly along the ground in blurry green, he thought, but it was very fast. His toes felt like jelly in his wet boots and he began to hear the river roaring.

Across the stream again he stepped out onto a wide gravel flat. A quiet pool echoed away from his right. The dog leaped in and swam around barking, sneezing with beech leaves sticking to his nose. The stream fell over a glassy slide into the river. His boots crunched on the quartz gravel and he began to see little tufts of gorse and broom in it, with occasional yellow flowers.

There was blackberry, he saw, and willow shooting, but between him and the river torrent crashing down a rapid stood a broad field of lupin with purple and red flower heads standing. He wanted to run in it. They must have come down the river, all these things from seeds carried willy-nilly by the miners to their claims and camps far up stream, carried by water and lodged in the flat after a flood, weeds that spread wherever men went.

He took huge breaths of the pollen and saw, at the water's edge, the trail of wild musk with its yellow antirrhinum flowers. He squatted and tasted watercress again. Wild mint trailed its pink roots below the clear surface. It would be a perfect place for fish. Beyond the lupins spray was flung up in the rapids. The sun caught it. He took off his boots and dried the soles of his feet on his trousers. Terns from the sea hunted the river. He wondered what they could be after but then he saw, in the slide, a thick shoal of elvers pressing into the stream as if nothing could stop them. He would camp there.

For two days he walked back on an inland route, braced against a bitter southerly gale with spring sleet, able to light a fire when he needed it but hardly sleeping until he reached his hut.

Dear Mr Henty,

I have met and talked at some length with Dr McIvor and I do not think that you should have any more concern for my earlier thoughts.

I have explored the stream as far as its mouth at the Taieri River and found the encroachment of weeds there quite disturbing. Floods must carry the seeds from the miners' camps at Ranfurly and Naseby, let alone what is carried in grasses for sheep.

I would be very much obliged if you could secure for me and send to me a balance or a set of scales. I suppose that gold assay scales would do. I must now measure and weigh the salmon smolt to assess their growth. There is now some urgency about this.

I consider the Deep Stream capital for salmon propagation if only the fish will return to the Taieri River after their release and their time spent feeding and growing in the ocean.

Dear Charlotte,
Thank you for the rose cutting and the other plants. I have put them in at my door along with my herbs which I hope to soon thin and plant out properly.

I have been down to the mouth of the Deep Stream on the Taieri River and found it a magical place although sadly being invaded by various weeds. They are making a lovely show of colour however and I made camp among them. Perhaps one day you would like to go there. I was very cold and wet coming back and often blessed you for giving me that coat. Please tell Gregory that salmon leave the stream and swim down to the sea where they grow into big fish before coming back to lay their eggs. Please say hullo to the monkey for me and to all the others. I am longing to see you all. I have also been out on the horses to look at sheep in a fog with Dr McIvor who is staying. He seems a very stern man and I do not know what he thinks of me. He seems to worry a lot about his daughter. I am glad you enjoyed the ball. The women told me about it and laughed that the men had to unhitch themselves from their sabres to dance even though they drank black velvet which I believe is stout and champagne together. I suppose you took that too. I hope Dan looked after you.

From the garden, Mary and Denebola brought him spring vegetables including a basket of the early pods of broad beans. He chopped up silver beet and baby white turnips and did not have enough pots or hooks over his fire to cook them all at once for a feast. Mary met him when he walked up to the house with the basket. She gave him a large package which had come and he knew that it must be the scales to weigh his fish. "What can that be?" She looked up at him and for the first time he noticed that she had dimples at the corners of her mouth which made her look very welcoming. "There must be people very fond of you in town." He decided that he would let her imagine that was true.

Somehow the smolt must be making changes to their bodies as they grew, that would make them able to enjoy salt water when they came to the sea. Carefully he unwrapped the scales, saving the brown paper and string and putting the white cardboard box aside. He looked at the scales on his table, their brass pans balanced delicately. Then he went to the bush and cut down a supplejack vine and a whippy shaft of lance wood. He took his flour bag kit and sewed it with string onto the vine bent in a circle and lashed to the shaft. He had a net. Then he put a little water into each of his pannikins and set them on the scales so that they were even, and stacked the brass weights into a cone.

He filled his billy with pond water and stood with the net sunk while he threw handfuls of liver meal out. The fish were writhing and they came closer, silver over the net as he threw. They were not afraid of him or his shadow. He lifted the net and caught three that flapped there, put them in the billy, slippery and bending, and took them inside. Once again he had to catch them. The puppies had been hard to catch. Their dark tawny fur had smelled of old meat and had felt slightly sticky. Their neck bones had pressed on his fingers as he twisted.

Now one fish squirmed in the pannikin and he measured its weight, stacking brass plugs on the other pan. It weighed just over an ounce. The other fish weighed two ounces and just over four and a half. They were inches long and he could still see the black skeleton. He put them back in the pond and pulled bidi-bid seeds from his socks that were scratching his ankles, broken seed heads that would drop wherever he washed. Growth. He had tried to play in the fives court at school, a twenty-feet-square place of polished stone with high plastered walls. The gutta percha ball hurt his hand when he hit it and made it hurt in the centre. Back and forth the ball went as he hit it and ran until the other boy knocked him over. He ran home with a grazed knee and his mother bandaged it and said that it would soon heal. When he picked the scabs one little drop of blood appeared. "Don't pick it," his mother said. He had never tried to play fives again.

The fish were instantly gone when he poured the billy back into the pond. He licked his finger where it had caught on the wire.

Albion sang a little to himself — the Ophelia song from *Hamlet*,

How shall I my true love know,
From another one?
By his cockle hat and staff
And his sandal shoon.

With his knife he cut a circle twenty inches across from the side of the scales box. He drew a cross on it. At the left arm of the cross he drew a square the shape of a Tarot card. Inside it he wrote 'Moral and Physical Health' and beside that, to the right of it, 1. HEALTH. Then, going counter clockwise around an inner circle, he wrote 2. HEART, 3. MONEY, 4. WORK. He repeated these words around the circle until they numbered twelve. Then he wrote in on the outer circle, on the card spaces after the first, 'Wealth, Acquisitions', 'Family and Friends', 'Property', 'Emotional Bonds', 'Illness', 'Husband, Colleague', 'Death, Inheritance, Gambling', 'Religious Beliefs', 'Profession', 'Friends, Help', and 'Misunderstandings, Ordeals'. Then he divided the whole circle in three, in groups of four, assigning counter-clockwise from the bottom into categories — 'Personal Problems', 'Family Problems', and 'Problems Concerning the Surroundings'.

At first the temptation was strong to try it on himself but he decided that he did not want to know. He wrapped the card carefully in paper. He remembered her insistent question to him: "Why do you carry the Tarot cards about with you if you don't believe what they say?" It wasn't just his mother although she had the gypsy fortune tellers to tea in her farmhouse kitchen. The gypsies also believed that if you drank baby's blood you would cure diseases and live forever but surely modern man had grown out of that. How would you keep up the supply of babies and in any case the Tarot was invented in Italian and Provençal households which were the refuge of magic and witchcraft which was much more archaic — and probably related to fungus growing on rye grass seed. "And I used to think my mother was a witch," he found himself saying.

He sighed. Unfortunately he was like everybody else and simply could not resist any chance, however implausible, of guessing at the future. Then he had to confess to himself that he carried the cards around because they'd appealed to women, whose idea of 'love' was essentially an idea of self-love — of love for clothes and cosmetics, of mirrors and scents, of the appearance of things. They liked to think of men looking at them and having satisfaction, never understanding that the act of overcoming emotions is the act of applying them to oneself and feeling what they do to oneself and understanding what that means.

He would take the Tarot circle to Charlotte at Christmas when Henty had said he could have a short holiday as long as he arranged for the fish to be fed.

A sweet scent came in his open door and he followed it to the bush, noticing that the trees had become alight with blossom. At the edge a great white daisy grew, with fleshy grey leaves close to the ground. Then there was a waxy yellow flower on a bare branch, drooping blossom on a native broom. He brushed against a lily, growing like tall grass with a white flower tipped in blue that fell off as he passed. Barclay had told him it was turutu. Then he found the scent which overwhelmed all the others, the blossom of the kohuhu, the colour of arterial blood. White blossom clotted the ribbon wood branches. A tui rustled its peacock wings in the hanging yellow bells of kowhai trees. Of all these, he took a branch of kohuhu up to the house.

"If you put this in your bedroom it will be strong in the stillness," he told Mary.

"Oh, but I can smell it from here. That is a wonderful gift, Mr Duffy. It is so much nicer than the smell of wool grease. I will put some in the parlour, too, and you may come and test it. You will come again?"

Suddenly he did not want her to be anxious. "Perhaps the flowers will soon drop," he said. "I had better come before they do." She was so young and clear.

"I suppose that Miss Denebola will be there too."

"I always like to have her by me."

Out at the meadow edges he found small orchids with fragile flowers or green hoods. He picked them carefully and pressed them between blotting paper under a book. He would make glue from sheep's feet, or egg white or flour and water, to paste them on sheets. Images of perfumed faces in the trees overwhelmed him.

He barely noticed, as he continued to weigh and measure in the heat, that Christmas had almost come. He packed a kit and asked Mr Barclay to drive him up to catch the coach. It would soon be the Summer Solstice, and Sirius was very bright in the sky at night.

Henry Jubes had driven his bullocks and waggon up McLaggan Street with a round and wide forest log. He unhitched his near side leader, a huge beast called Prince, from the chains and shackled him to the log.

"He'll do anything," Henry said. "He'll pull it off like yanking out a tree stump. He's so great I can let him off anywhere and he'll go straight home to his manger for his hay. He'll lift the latch on the stable doors with his nose and just walk in. He's that knowing."

The log fell to make the street shake but Price dragged it through the stableyard gates and out onto the washing green.

"It's the Yule Log," Charlotte said. "Dolly and Mavis will light it and keep it alive with coals, tonight on Christmas Eve, and they'll keep it going until Twelfth Night. That's the old Scottish tradition and I'm keeping it now. I know it's in the open air even though it's Christmas but the days are so long now. Something about it, well, of the noble savage, I think. We even have a baby holly tree in the garden."

Albion wondered if her calendar and her folklore were a little awry but grinned and watched the log settled clear of the washing line on which the monkey swung in some kind of delight in the hot evening air.

"And some red mistletoe on the silver beech up the gully," Dan said.

"Pirirangi," said Albion, feeling wise. "It is in flower, too."

"A fine soup," Thora said, lifting her spoon as they began to eat at three in the afternoon the next day.

"I caught the blue cod off the rocks at Lawyers Head," Dan said. "Then I simmered it for a long time with some of the old potatoes that were left and an onion beginning in the garden. Then I sieved it. And I caught a dog fish but when I put my knife through its head a tiny dog fish swam out of its belly and slithered away down the pools."

"Viviparous," Albion said. "Producing live young. Some fish seem to do that."

They ate goose with new potatoes, parsnips and spring cabbage, and a bowl of gravy that Dolly said was her 'special' and some red currant jelly she had made a year before from a dripping bag and kept. Then there was suet pudding with currants and raisins, brown with molasses.

"Yvonne is allowed to put on the cognac," Charlotte said. "I don't see why the men have to do everything." The blue flames rose.

Gregory found a sixpence buried there and was the lucky one, they said. Dan said he had found the raspberries in a patch of canes left behind in the Leith Valley and Henry admitted that he had filched the strawberries from a garden at Palmerston, carting them home afraid they would ripen too fast.

"Whose bath night is it?" Charlotte asked when they sat back.

"Mine, I think," said John Wilkes. "But I'm going to break up the salty rocks with a hammer a bit so they'll dissolve more. Perhaps they could go in a muslin wrap. There's some old flour mill stones on the wharf, come from Australia, and I often wonder if they could be used for the bath salts but you'd have to put them under cover in case it rained, and a steam engine to turn them. Expensive."

"Bath salts. The very name. 'Charlotte's Bath Ambrose'. I could call them that — in a little bag."

"Mind they don't make the bath too slippery," said Thora. "But it is true. We must all keep clean, even if it is Christmas."

"The hot and cold water must mix much like Dr Kelvin has discovered gases do," Albion said, slightly fuddled at the table cloth. "And Dr Glausious has discovered how everything tends to disorder and it has been termed 'entropy' just a few years ago. Heat flows into cold. It is always the same. Dr Kelvin has called it a Law."

"Oh tush! That's very complicated. I find that my piano is hard enough. Miss Yates has been getting me to play from Bach's forty-eight preludes and fugues. She says the key to it is in a piece in Book II. I have memorised the notes. They go C G E C A F G in a kind of waltz time but of course the waltz had not been invented then."

"We all move to a kind of waltz," John Wilkes said, a little peevishly. "You can hear it in a steam engine. That's what is wrong with Julius Vogel. He wants to build railway lines but he is unable to hear the music. And that Sir George Grey — he was once hit in the thigh with a spear flung by an Australian Aboriginal warrior and now he thinks he is a god."

"But that doesn't mean that I haven't got a good idea," Charlotte said. The excited blood was in her face.

"Mother — will you be able to play songs for me soon? You are always saying that I have been given a good voice."

"Vocal cords," Albion thought aloud. "Where do vocal cords come from? Do the birds have any?"

Charlotte appeared in her mud on Boxing Day. He could hardly believe that such a greenish mask could make her eyes so keen. She looked straight at him and he felt in touch with her soul, if there was such a thing. The mud was like wood, like a domino. Her hair was stiff with bits of it.

"Don't look so worried. It just peels off and I feel good."

"Mother! Why do you have to do that all the time?"

"Hush. Because it is good for my skin. It would be good for all ladies who grow too old, or ladies who have to live in too much sun."

"But I like our skin, anyway. How can it be improved? That is a new word I have learned."

"There is salt in sweat and in tears," Albion said in general. "The question is, how do we make sure that we have the right amount of salt in our bodies and how do we get rid of it if we have too much?"

"Perhaps the mud can take out the salt and that's why it works," Gregory added.

"Whatever happens, I have a good idea," Charlotte said. She went to the piano and down the hall he could hear her start to sing.

Westering home with a song in the air,
Light i' the eye and it's goodbye to care,
Laughter o' love and a welcoming there,
Isle o' my heart my own one."

"That was a Bonnie Prince Charlie song. He was a Royal baby. Then they spirited him away in a boat," Gregory whispered. Charlotte was playing with both hands.

He went out and the Yule Log was smouldering over the Brighton coal.

Knowing that he had little time left, Albion went walking by himself. He walked slowly up High Street to Manse Street. There was a spring of fresh water there, where once the fire engines had been filled, and now there was a public drinking fountain with a jet coming out of the chromed top. He waited in a line while people drank from it. When it was nearly his turn he saw, bending in front of him, a brightly coloured parasol. She turned towards him, shaking drops from her rouged mouth. A purple scarf covered her neck and her breasts where they were pushed up by her yellow satin bodice.

"I look after a salmon hatchery. What do you do?" He had no power over the impulse.

"I paint parasol covers." She slowly turned the parasol above her. Light fell through it.

"Like that one?"

"I make them, too. I pattern them. Where are your fish?"

"They're all in a pond up in the hills. Would you like to walk with me? My name is Albion Duffy."

"I am Jean. And yes, I could walk with you. Is not the sun very hot and no wind." Men and women in worn clothes parted for them to let them pass. She took his arm as though they were old friends. At her room in an old wooden building she showed him how she cut parasol covers out of pale silk and stitched their folds to fit on the ribs, cut frills for their edges and the cap over the ferrule. Pots of paint were lined against a wall, with the smell of linseed oil. Brushes stood in water. Palettes were blotched with colour.

"I can sell a few covers here but I send them up to Wellington and Auckland too. The makers seem to want them more and more." She sat on her bed and pulled off her scarf. "I can't make you tea. There's no fire in the kitchen until the end of the day."

They became covered in sweat. Her body was round and firm. She was short and as he lay over her he did not think, as he felt her skin against him and the little pains in his nipples, that he should worry about cleanness. The smell of linseed became part of his ardour.

"Phew. It must have been a long time for you," she finally said. "I would like to start again." He slid down on her skin. As he looked up at them her breasts seemed to be like rainbow colours spreading in a film across still water, drops of nectar oil. He waited for her hand on the long muscle deep between his open thighs. Coloured light shone through the parasol covers drying on a line at her window. Her brown eyes had become topaz. "I have never felt like this. It is so sudden. Don't you think that there must be something watching over us? I read books and I think there must be something in the stars. Don't you think there are magic things? Yes. Like that."

"All I know is, when I saw you by the fountain, we had to be like this. Perhaps it was the sun?"

"I go swimming. I swim in the sea when I can."

"Are you a mermaid then?"

"Touch me. Can you feel scales? And is my tail sewn up?" After a time she said, "Look. I have a mirror like a mermaid. And I can give you an apple although they are green yet." Then, "Do you believe that the dead come back — come back in us?"

"I don't think I believe in reincarnation. Is that what you mean? If I am reincarnated now it is because I feel whole with you for some reason."

"Have we fallen in love, so suddenly? Does that explain the spirit feeling? There are so many books now, and people like to think about strange forces about us, something more grand than us. Bigger. That seems to swirl about. I am so sure that it comes out in my painting."

"All I know is that I feel that you clean me. You make me feel risen up. And that is very strange after so short an acquaintance." Then he felt afraid. "Do you do this often? Is this the first time?"

"Believe me. This has never happened to me before. You must not think I am that kind of girl."

"I don't," he said. "I truly don't. But I have to go back to my fish tomorrow."

"I'll wait. Believe me I'll wait. The time will pass and you will come back. I will watch the stars. I will get incense and burn it for you. I will watch the smoke. I am sure that it will come out in my painting." He could see the folds in her belly when she sat, making dark lines which he did not like.

"Tell me about this parcel," Charlotte said. "I have unwrapped it and you have made this card with many things on it. Is it for me to do my Tarot?" She seemed to be entirely engaged with herself, Albion thought, but he sat down with her at the elephant table in the evening. "You've had an adventure," she said. "I can see it in you," and Dan had said that he smelled of some paint. "I don't care. You're just a young man. But we do care about the cards, don't we." It was a statement and seemed to him to be stern, as if she had set her mind to it. But he made sure that she let her energy flow into the pack of cards when he handed them to her, shuffled them from right to left and cut them over the spread circle.

Then he took the cards and laid them out, one at a time around the squares that he had drawn and named. He wondered if there was anything of the charlatan in him and realised that he had never thought that before. He began to draw the cards, placing them one after another on the twelve spaces. He went around the circle five times and had six cards left. "Now tell me which areas of the three around the outside that you are thinking about most."

"Mostly about things to do with me. And about things around me."

He laid the six cards within the segments marked 'Personal Problems' and 'Problems Concerning the Surroundings'.

"I thought you might have been concerned about family things," he said and smiled at her.

"Not so much." She was definite. "Now go on — turn them up and tell me."

He was interrupted by the thought of Jean, and then, immediately, that weeds must have started growing long ago in the corners of the Queen's Crystal Palace, the beams of which were raised by horse labour.

He started, feeling pessimistic, turning up the cards in the section of her surroundings.

"Now remember that you were riding in the Chariot and that, through your Death card, you are going through the process of change."

He revealed, over religious beliefs, the five of Cups, then over profession, the Wheel of Fortune, the nine of Clubs over help from friends, and the Princess of Clubs over her ordeals. Under the Wheel of Fortune the card was the three of Swords.

"Look at that." He felt himself growing more generous.

Boys and girls come out to play,
The moon doth shine as bright as day.
Leave your supper and leave your sleep
And let's go dancing in the street.

She sang the last two lines softly. "But I don't understand what it means."

"The Wheel," he said, "means that you will have success in what you choose to do but under it is suggested that while money transactions will be honest there may be mischief, perhaps even quarrelling and strife. But never mind, the nine of Clubs proposes that you will have great strength. But it can't be all good. There is disappointment there in what you are going to believe, and as an ordeal the Princess of Clubs makes an entrance — a young woman with gold hair and blue eyes who wants power and I see another woman with dark yellow eyes."

What was going on, he wondered? The blue-eyed woman was clearly Mary but she could also turn out to be cruel and domineering. The topaz-eyed one that had drifted into his vision did not belong in the spread and he understood the idea of Jean as coming from himself.

Jean had had a cat, he had seen that in a flash at her door, and he should have said, when she talked about spirits, something like "Spiritualism is rife these days. Our greatest poets practise it. Old ladies in back streets attract seances as if they were abortionists." Suddenly he counted himself worthless for indulging in the Tarot. He was losing his own account of himself.

"Forgive me — my own concerns sometimes intrude upon your legitimate inquiries." For her personal problems he turned up the Magician for her property — "that's wisdom and handling care with skill" — the crown of his hat with the brim bent into a kind of figure eight on its side was yellow. His sleeves were yellow and the ground he stood on. The two of Swords (quarrels made up), was under it for money and an assured gain, and the Prince of Clubs told that somebody who was just and generous would enter her life and she would be healthy because she would not be mean.

"I suppose I had better be brave and look at my family problems," she said. Her emotions were coloured by the Hanged Man, with the four of Clubs under it, the eight of Clubs affected her heart, the nine of Coins promised her money, but the 8 of Cups over work promised an interest that would be sometimes unstable. She had undergone a punishment but her heart was filled with so much energy that the only word for it was electrical. She would give off sparks.

"I doubt if you have anything very much to worry about," he said when she looked doubtful and confused. "The thing to remember is, I think, that courage is an over-riding emotion — it puts all our other functions into abeyance. The Tarot teaches us about compensation, about taking all our resources into our notice." Then he found himself exclaiming, "I'll give you some money! I'll give you three hundred pounds if you need it."

"It's not that," she said, sweeping up the cards and looking away at the blue lion. "Oh I suppose it is, in a way. I'm not really worried about Gregory even though I still often think of his father. And Mr Lancaster is very kind, letting me live here and giving me an allowance. But I spend too much, I know, and I will have to take care. I will have to find a way of making an income for myself and I do not really know what to do."

Albion felt stronger. The lion seemed to be smiling at him and looked almost green in the lamp light. "Don't worry about the Hanged Man — it just means that you have suffered through no fault of your own."

"But I did. I gave in to him, didn't I, and I am still paying the price. I always will."

"I hesitate to ask, but to whom did you give in — the father of your child or Mr Lancaster who gives you support?"

"Oh both, damn it. Forgive me. I am vexed by all this. I didn't mean to use bad language. And even Logan Salpetreux — I gave in to him, too. I am so weak, I think."

"I'm sure you are not weak. I am endlessly impressed by the way you have organised your life."

"But if he hadn't given me a lion and the monkey to remember him by I don't know what I would have done. It was those things that kept me going — things from him. I don't know how I kept the monkey or fed him and he even slept in the same bed as we did when Gregory was small. The two of us had to keep him warm and I don't know how we did it." She began to cry.

"Look at everything you've got here. Give thanks."

"What to? I'm starting to wonder if I can believe in anything at all. And you are going back to your fish."

"Not before I have been to the bank for you. You will feel better."

"Oh, I suppose that I am lucky. I just have to believe in that."

He stood. "Lucky Charlotte," he said and touched her arm across the table.

He had not been entirely frank with the Tarot, he thought. He had not pulled down all the stacks of cards and examined all of them. That would have to wait for another time and meanwhile would he have found there things that were deeply disturbing to himself, questions asked to which he did not know the answer, collisions of feeling and argument that would upset him?

He was just as bad as a seance woman and he did not even believe in what he had done. Women liked Tarot because of their peculiar view of authority. For them authority was a collection of opinions expressed by a group of women, in this case represented by the cards, and a man obtained authority by seeming to represent the collective view.

EIGHT

Resolution seemed to come to him with Deep Stream. Here was Mary, the fair-haired Princess of Clubs, among the bush flowers that still had some fragrance, beside the pond where the fish leapt to the surface when he threw in the first handful of meal. He wanted it to go on for ever and nothing seemed to stand in his way. When he put his finger in the water a little fish came immediately and nibbled at it softly like the eel had done.

"My father is coming again soon," Mary said one day. He was uncertain because she would not look at him. She held a parasol and revolved it slowly.

"There will be plenty of news, I suppose," Denebola said. They were in the vegetable garden where he was picking some of the first peas. The earth was soft between the rows.

"Will you be having anything to say to him?" Mary spoke almost in a whisper. The pods seemed to rattle.

"There are many things on my mind," he said. "I will look forward to talking with him."

"Don't you think you should discuss it with Mary first,"

Denebola said. She was so forthright that he asked how the lettuce was coming on instead but then she moved away. All his skin prickled. It was time that he spoke but it would mean that he undertook a commitment.

"Mary . . . my fish are growing in the pond and I have been thinking about my future here."

"Yes?"

"And I have been wondering if you would think of making something more permanent out of . . . all this."

"I am sure that I would be very happy to. I have admired you a great deal from the beginning and I am sure that I would find happiness with you."

"You are very young and I . . ."

"I do not think that you should let that worry you. I am well able to dispose of myself, I think."

"Then . . . I am asking you if you will . . ."

"Then I have agreed, have I not . . . Albion."

For the first time she had said his name and he felt very proud of it. His shadow was thick beneath him, bearing him up in the high sun, and she looked directly at him under her parasol and the shade that darkened her eyes. "We shall wait to hear from my father," she said.

"You have made me feel very safe. I have wanted to feel safe. It is very safe being here. I like it."

That was why he had done it, he thought — because it made him feel safe, and everything else in the world — Charlotte, Jean, everything — was so uncertain. He could be a father, he thought, and felt himself rise to the picture of the water on her. He would not be afraid, no, he would enjoy that, it would seem like being fulfilled after all. There was a joy he had not expected. He wished that his mother was alive to learn of it. He buttoned his waistcoat firmly.

Although he had hardly thought about it he had changed his state. It was as if the heavens had opened and even the sun was more bright. He found himself grinning at her. He was without doubt at last. How extraordinary that among all the confusion of people he had met, of things which he had found his body doing without thought, he should be given certainty, the solution which removed the past and gave him a new life.

"You seem to have come to some conclusion," Denebola said, coming up to them. "I always wondered when you played at dominoes, if it was ordained. And I brought you hot wine then." She laughed.

"Yes," they said together. Mary gave him a sponge cake with a crusty, sugary top that she said she had baked slowly in a billy at a corner of the flame.

Albion lifted the books from the front of his fireplace with the blotting paper in which orchids were pressed. The past did not seem real any more. The dog looked sideways at him as if testing his resolve.

A hot and dry wind came from the north-west one morning when Dr McIvor arrived. It still blew when the cowman called and asked him to go to the house. It was as if his stomach first heard this news. He felt a lowness there as if he had been hit but he restored himself in thinking that the right hour had come. He was armed as he went to the doctor with the might of his daughter's wishes. He began to smile, only half aware of himself, hesitant but on a mission, armed with right. "Wipe that smile from your face," he heard his father say, and his mother would have said, "Now, Mr Duffy, do not be too hard on him." Perhaps his chest was indeed puffed up, as it was said happened to people who believed in what they were doing, and perhaps his knees did feel strange, as if they could hardly put his feet straight in front of him, as was said too, but he was strong, was he not, and he would go on as the emmisary.

Clouds were huge in the south-west and growing black. It would be raining in the tussock lands behind. The stream would soon begin to rise. He tried to breathe deeply and evenly as he walked but his toes met small, confusing stones. His mother had heard a man speak who said that he walked a mile every day with his palms turned out to catch the sun, breathing deeply through his nose and looking up. He had written it down in a magazine so that other people would know. Albion counted regularly now as he filled his chest and let it go in a rhythm. He had the authority on all sides and must not be afraid. Mary guided him through the kitchen. "Be strong," she whispered.

He stood tall but Dr McIvor, upright in front of the mantelpiece even though it was too hot for a fire told him to sit down. Sunlight from the parlour window hurt his eyes. I have been manouvered already, he thought as the other man became a blur. What if the man were ordinary in spite of this, what if he had peeling skin between his toes sweating in his socks, what if his scrotum itched, what if he had cut himself when he shaved, what if he wished that he had not pulled on a vest under his shirt, over his bones that carried his flesh?

"A very hot wind, is it not?"

"Yes, sir. I think it may rain in the end."

"And the fish, will they be comfortable in a flood?"

"I have taken precautions. The Society has been very prompt in sending me equipment that I discovered I had need of."

"We have good men, I think. And you seem to be one."

"Sir, I have talked with your daughter . . . She is . . ."

"But the trouble is we have come upon hard times. The Central Government has been making a money contribution to the work of the Society but I have learned, through my elected position in Wellington, that this is to be discontinued. The effort must go into railways."

"I have spoken to Miss McIvor and asked . . ."

"And that being so the Society which is almost entirely supported by contributions from men such as myself, has found itself in a situation of some embarassment if it is to continue its work."

"And she has agreed with me that next spring . . ."

"And so it is with great regret that the Society has decided that I myself, with my staff here, must take up the care of the salmon pond."

"But I have made arrangements with your daughter . . ."

"And since that is the case the Society has no other option but to terminate your employment here."

"It would be convenient to both of us if . . ."

"The committee has decided that it can continue your emolument for the rest of this month only."

"Does that mean . . ."

"I am sure that you will soon find other employment and you can be assured of being provided with an excellent reference. I am disturbed to be the bringer of such news but I am sure that you will understand the Society's position."

"Dr McIvor, does that mean that Miss McIvor will not . . ."

"If you are unable to take all your equipment with you I am sure that Mr Barclay will be able to send it on to you. I presume that you will have the same address at Mr Lancaster's house."

Dr McIvor, full of politeness, showed him to the front door so that he could step out into the garden, where, so long ago, he had found Mr Barclay scything grass without his collar.

Albion sat at his table with his knees together, shaking. The dog put his chin there, looking up as if yearning, with his ears back. He did not have the power to stroke its head. The enormity of what McIvor had said towered over him. He was right. The man was a bully. Carlyle had said that Napoleon Bonaparte failed because he thought men were dupable. That monster had said, when he planned his disaster in Russia, that he didn't care if he lost a million men fighting there. Albion's own mother and father had been brought up under the threat of the 'bogey-man', as England thought of Napoleon, and now McIvor was trying to do the same thing to him. He had promised the earth and was now giving nothing, a spectre of the bogey bully, the maniac who was the consequence of human belief.

When an end came to the afternoon, Albion loaded his gun. He laughed bitterly to himself because there was nothing else left.

At the edge of the pond heart's-ease plants had crept down to the damp soil by the bullrushes. He picked a withered flower that was still blooming. Westerly light was yellow under the cloud. It made a prismatically lit half-world in which he shot four hunting white-faced herons. He waded in the water to retrieve their bodies and laid them on the bending stems of blue. He noticed buds. He could hear the rising stream beginning to rush in the pond race.

He went back to his hut, dug his tarragon and put it in a bag. It would keep only if the roots were kept damp with earth. He stuffed clothes in his kit. He closed an open copy of *The Mill on the Floss* lying on his table.

Lightning began at dark, over the rising stream. He took up his mattock in the dark and stumbled, almost crawling at times, in the rain that had begun but was lit by the flashes, to the end of the pond. He picked away heavily at the posts which held up the dam gates. "That's for Mary!" he yelled to the night. "You can know death and expect it, Mary." Soon the posts crumbled out of the shingle. "This is for the living. It's unknown . . . but it must be full of promise!" He heaved them out and away, hearing the water begin to rush. "Pray to God the fish are in it. Pray to God they will find the sea. Pray to God they are not too small for the journey. Pray to God for their safety. Oh God, I hope that they can grow."

He tied the dog at his door in the sudden cold and began to walk towards the hill with his kit bag and his gun on his shoulders. Rain ran from his oilskin jacket, soaking his thighs, and fell in streams from his sou-wester, silvery in the lightning. The dog yelped in a scream between the thunder. He was overwhelmed with his feelings at leaving. He screamed back at the dog. "Women's love is self-loving junk anyway, and your Dr McIvor doesn't seem to understand that!" He could hear his boots sucking the grass. Perhaps Dr McIvor understood it too well.

"But you have become engaged," Charlotte said when he knocked on her door. "You are going to marry. Thora told me. She is making a dress for a lady who visited your place and learned of it there."

"Well, I am not any more," Albion said. Women always talked. The town knew everything that happened.

"Oh come in. I haven't let your room yet. You can still have it back if you want." The pond would be quite drained, the mud flats bare. He was glad that he had remembered to knock over the scarecrows.

Mary wrote to him:

Dear Mr Duffy,
My father has told me of the devastation you have caused and I have seen it. I have seen too the bodies of the poor little birds that you shot so cruelly, that my father had brought so full of hope from Australia.

I am deeply sorry to have to tell you that I can no longer honour the understanding which we had come to. But I do wish you well, Albion, and will always hold dear the memory of our being together. I have arranged for Mr Barclay to have your equipment packed and sent on to you.

He did not reply to her, believing that he had nothing more to say than his actions.

He played with Gregory and the monkey after school. "Look. I have learned a new word," Gregory said. "It is 'REFUSE'. It means that you decide not to have something that you have seemed to want." Albion felt his heart twist with shame but instead he showed Gregory how to measure the height of a tree in the garden by holding up a card and striding out the distance from the trunk. The monkey ran up the tree and he laughed for the first time.

Elegant Cheng greeted them when they went for supper. "New words have found," he said. "Think calling poem. It go, 'No strength in east wind. It fade one hundred flowers. Not many road here to place where people live for ever. Little bird come. It bring letter. I ask for letter from you.' Ah, and 'moonlight cold on me', it say. I have new lamb tonight. You like?"

"What will you do now?" Charlotte asked.

"'Ye banks an' braes o' bonnie Doon,' " Albion said. "'*How can ye bloom sae fresh a' fair?*' I don't know yet. Life seems to be passing me by."

With his tongue he felt a hair sticking to the roof of his mouth. He took it out and inspected his fingers. They were wet with saliva. He rubbed them on his coat and scratched the table cloth.

"But you could do anything. You have so many qualities. The town is crying out for people who can turn their hands to many things — like making things or teaching. We have so few teachers."

"It is all very well to have that opinion. I am flattered by it. But I have thought that women have made themselves victims because they take easily to the group and I suppose that I do not do that. It seems to me that women pay no fee for their transport by the inventiveness of men. Mary McIvor was probably like that, waiting for her father's say in everything. Men always accept that kind of thinking and decide that they are needed while women continue to have the illusion of forward progress that is without fetters, if you like. But I suppose that that is concerned with their ability to decide to have babies. I don't mean to offend you — but women seem to make themselves hysterical and inferior through this." He paused. "Of course it is regrettable that some men take advantage of it — to indulge in such pastimes as the modern quackery of patent medicine."

"You must talk to Dan, I think. It is time that you talked to men again."

"I wish that it was as easy as that. I am a failure now. I have ruined everything that I had. I was beginning to build something but I have thrown it all away. I thought that I had a future."

He showed Gregory how to step through a playing card, a feat which the boy thought was impossible but Albion showed him that, by making cuts around the card in a square spiral, he could open it out and pass it over his body. "That's magic," Gregory said. The monkey began to play with the slivered piece and tore it up.

"Dan," he said. "Tell me about the desert."

"But that was twenty-five years ago. I've nearly forgotten."

"How could you forget?"

"Well, I will never forget the heat. It got up to a hundred and eighteen degrees and we had no water. The sheep nearly died, and my dog, and the bullocks got covered in blood in their yokes, pulling in soft sand with the iron tyres falling off the wheels they shrank so much."

"Why did you go?"

"Well, in 1843 there was a lot to find out about Australia. Old Captain Sturt, he had been with the Duke of Wellington on the Spanish Peninsula when the French were being rolled up before Napoleon was smited at Waterloo in Belgium back in 1815. He used to paint in water colours. He got very rude about the birds I skinned for him and said they wouldn't stuff properly for his museum. It was a mess — they hadn't brought all the right things for a year in the wilderness and the rations were cut every few weeks even though we had to build cairns out of huge stones, and walk. We only just came back alive."

"Charlotte said I should talk to you."

"She's a canny woman, Albion. I've always thought, you know, that a lot of thought burdened you. That was my trouble, too, I think. Burdened with thought."

"But Dr McIvor is a fool. All he has got is power to pull strings in the Government and that's how I got sacked. He doesn't know anything about salmon. The fish would have died. I had to let them go."

"There was the girl, too."

"I was thrown against her. I thought . . ."

"You're just young, I'd say. You've got to try, that's all it is."

John Wilkes got him a job. He knew little about steam engines but there was a post for an oiler to the steam engine on a pile driver working in the harbour. At first he had to help shape the piles, long hardwood gum trunks that had been brought from Tasmania. They were to go in a row in the water so that decking could be placed and the land filled in behind it. At home he had learned skill with an adze to shape the wood. A point had to be made and covered with iron riveted in and then a chamfer cut in the head for an iron band to be shrunk on so that it did not split with the driving. Then he had to row out to the barge in the coal boat and learn how to drip oil onto the connecting rods, the gear wheels, pins and sheaves that led power from the pistons to the rotating clutch winch, and grease the wire ropes. He grew used to the rhythmic thump of the steel driver on the pile when it was wound up and let go. He heard the sound as he tried to sleep. It engulfed him and he was always dirty with coal soot and oil. His back grew corded from emptying coal sacks for the boiler in the wind that seemed to blow for ever down the harbour. Then he felt that life was becoming too certain, faces too familiar.

"I have to go and live by myself. I have to find another lodging," he told Charlotte one Sunday.

"But who will look after you? How will you eat?"

"I'll be all right. I've just got to go. I wish I could explain it."

He found a room in a terrace house in Manor Place. A Lebanese tinker owned the house and was often away with his donkey cartload of cottons and ribbons and saucepan patches. Church spires seemed to be rising everywhere in the town as he wandered one Sunday afternoon with his muffler wound around his neck because of the rain and cold. He saw her umbrella first, in bright oil colours, and then, as he drew nearer, her steady eyes underneath, her round face and slightly Roman nose, her pale brown skin.

"You are making umbrellas now, I see. Indeed the weather has been wet."

"Oh Albion, I have seen you about so many times but you are always with a lady and I am too afraid to talk to you. But I knew I would meet you. It is in my smoke."

The look of her wooden house made him feel good, the granular texture of it which seemed almost edible and when he went up her stairs he would come to the hall door with its design of blue, green and red glass, the gateway to another wooden hall with her door. It was cold and he bought her coal for the fireplace where there was a cast iron hob. He bought a large iron pot to put on it with water. They walked to the Caversham Valley where Dr McIvor kept his town house, to Lake Logan where the harbour invaded vast mud flats at high water, where hundreds of black-backed gulls roosted on the fertile mud when it was there, unlike the little red-billed gulls that always fluttered around his pile driver, in and out of the smoke. They walked to Anderson's Bay, along a rough track made by men who had dug a ditch and flung up the spoil for a place to walk, making themselves thin to pass girls and boys who came with full milk pails swinging on shoulder yokes. He saw Dan, one day, in a parade of the volunteer regiment in their finery, and returned his wave. The pipe band played and hounds passed up the valley following an aniseed trail left by a huntsman in red. He marvelled at how green the hills were because leaves did not fall from the trees in winter.

The little bones at the top of his neck cracked and she no longer said, as she rubbed him, "Your back feels like concrete." He did not have headaches or pains in his knees. At night he could see that the planet Venus was close to the Moon and wondered if he could believe in love or if there was nothing more to expect than the tempest of good feelings that came in bed. Sometimes he would hear a small noise between her legs.

"Stinkweed," he said as she fanned the blankets. "Stinkwood. Hupirau-ririki. Mr Barclay showed me in the bush. It has beautiful red berries but it smells of outhouses. It's a beautiful little tree. That's strange, isn't it."

She cuddled close to him and he stroked her hair.

"Stoke up the fire," she said. "We can have a wash. I'm all sticky."

He poured the pot full of hot water into a wooden tub and

then cooled it with water from downstairs, hoping as he went that any ardour he had left would not be cooled away. It was soon revived in the soap as he stood while she poured warm water down him and played with him in the slipperiness until he begged her to let him dry himself first, not knowing why he wanted so much to do this when they could have been close just wet and standing up.

Afterwards he took her guiltily to Elegant Cheng's, hoping that they would not be interrupted. Cheng looked puzzled. "I still have poem," he said. "More than thousand year olt.'Boat sail in night like your boat to driving. Stars falling down. Mast is, how is it, like steep tiled roof. Then all flat. Nothing to see. All quick very high moon. Poem say, what I am. I am heaven. I am earth. I am one seagull float on water. Is all made of heavens.' I bring you duck with cabbage."

"Is that all we are — just a little speck of a seagull in the Universe?"

"But we feel. We have things together, don't we? I believe in spiritual things, don't you? I've tried so hard to teach you."

"Dan says that out in the desert the Australian aboriginals find a kind of grass. They beat little seeds out of it and they grind them between stones into a kind of oily paste and eat it. There's almost no water but he saw a woman giving her breast to a puppy dog."

"The spirits always find a way, you see."

"Well, my spirit will be weak if we don't go now and I must not be late for work."

One evening they stood naked in front of each other before her fire. He saw the rose on her belly. He grabbed a paint brush, dipped in her pot of red paint and scrawled a star on her skin. The brush spattered on the floor.

"Ha!" he said. "You talk about the spirits all the time. I suppose deep down you believe in God. The Christian God raised you. Was not that so? You believe in that primitive and vulgar Christian sacrifice, do you? In the expression of the desire to kill that all men have? Men and women have always clung to it, especially women. Men just do the killing. *God!* The most pernicious and destructive idea that man ever came up with."

She was crying. She grabbed the brush, and pressing it to herself painted a cross.

"That's just words. What are words then? Tell me what love is, tell me what music is!" She yelled at him.

"Words? We learn them at the breast from noises we make to get food. And music — that is pure emotion. People think they can find god in it anytime just because it makes them feel good. The Arabs have the whirling dervishes and while the Arab music plays they turn round and round until they feel giddy and because of this derangement of their senses they think and say they are feeling god. That's what music is — a feeling that people call spiritual because either it makes them feel good or they don't know enough to explain it."

"And love? And jealousy?"

"Now there you've hit it. The marshalling of all your resources in order to mate, to make another animal, and then you feel panic at the thought of this chance being taken away and you give it the elevated name of 'jealousy'."

"Oh, get out! Go away now. I don't want to hear any more of your lies. You're the devil. And I've got the cross on me. See?"

He walked back to Manor Place and his cold bed. Charlotte had sent him a letter.

NINE

Dear Albion,
I have determined to take an expedition. I feel that I cannot leave without you. I need your help. Everybody else is willing to help but I need you. Henry is taking his bullock team which I need for carriage and Dan comes too. I wrote to Grigori in care of his mother and father in Basle and he has sent me, as I asked, a wicker hamper with four large flasks of flower oils in it. They are to perfume the bath rocks and the mud. Grigori did not know that he was a father. Imagine that. He now has another lady and seven more children. He is the captain of a tug boat on the Rhine River. I also wrote to Mr Lancaster care of his agent here with whom I always deal. He is in San Fransisco and is willing to arrange shipping space. He has also given me the names of shopkeepers who will sell my wares when I have prepared them.

That being so, I have to go on the expedition to get more supplies of the rocks and mud that Logan told me about. They are far away in Central Otago but Henry says that he is not deterred and Dan agrees that it is less than two weeks' journey to the mud and even less to where Logan has marked the presence of the rocks above the river gorge to the west of the Dunstan mountains, not far up the river from Dunstan the town itself. We can easily get the rocks and mud and it would be of great value to have you with us for help. You will come, won't you? I have even kept your room, you know, if you would have it until we go.

It would be spring before long, Albion thought, feeling exhausted by his thoughts. Nothing could be better for him now than a journey. But what if he should die while undertaking it? He had no will, had made no provision for what happened to his property if he were to die. In his bare room he took a sheet of paper and his pen and wrote slowly:

"I, Albion Duffy, being of sound mind, do hereby leave my worldly goods to Gregory Brosnahan. I appoint as my executor Daniel Cockle or a man to be chosen by him should he be unable to carry out this duty."

He wrote the date on it and signed it. But what, he wondered, would it be like to die? The thought filled him with fear.

I must use my resources and ask of myself the question that I have trained myself to ask. Why am I feeling these feelings at this time?

He believed in the protestations he had made to Jean about not believing in the 'human spirit'. While he still felt flayed, that was the word, his skin stripped off, by her reply, he had to accept that he had said what he had said. Skin. The Romans had been careful, at their baths, to have a slave rub them with an abrasive so that pieces of dead skin were taken off. They reported feeling made clean by bathing.

And if the outer layer of skin died, then so all the parts of a man within the skin would die, no matter how it was pampered with breathing and food and drink or the pouring forth of seed. Death would then be simply 'deadness' and a state that he could not imagine because he could not imagine what it would be like to have no consciousness of himself. His consciousness must be the result of the activities of all of his body parts that were alive, a result of his whole body being live. Fear must be the way those organs responded to the thought that he would not, in death, have consciousness of himself. So it did not matter that his fellow men and women had surrounded themselves with food and drink, companionship and comfort in order not to feel this fear. Fear was something that just happened and he would accept it as part of life. That being so he could teach himself not to have this fear and could accept that he was alone. He began to feel a sense of pleasure. I can live with that, he thought, no matter what other people try to put into words about it.

With any good chance in the lottery of life, the random and accidental coming together of all the things that made his body, Gregory would inherit many useful qualities from his mother and father as well as money. How he would use such gifts was completely unknowable and if Albion were to die on this journey he could die happily, knowing that knowledge would be of no further use to him. Should his body be burned up in the way the Indians did so that it became some ashes and some gas that went into the sky, or should he be put into the ground to decompose and help the trees and flowers and vegetables to grow? On the whole, he thought, the result would be the same. Whatever it was that he was made of would go back to an arrangement of life which had meant that he had been conceived and born in the first place. There was not the slightest need for the idea of any spiritual plan or intervention, and Gregory would find that out for himself according to his lights. And if he died, Dan and

Henry and Charlotte would be there with him. He would not lack the power of being certain. He decided that he would prefer to be burned even though any thought for such a desire could not be justified.

Henry called on him to play cribbage. He brought out the scoring board with holes in it that had ivory pegs and a well-used pack of cards. "And one for his Nob!" he would cry triumphantly as he added up the value of his hand and counted the Jack and moved a peg on the holes. Dan went to the town Arsenal where he was allowed because he was a Volunteer, and brought back dozens of gunpowder bags made of canvas coated with rubber to keep damp out. Yvonne made sun hats for them all after carefully measuring the sizes of their heads. She made them out of white cotton heavily stitched to stiffen them. Thora made patterns for shirts and trousers according to size and had them made up in blue denim that had been invented on the California goldfields.

In these warm early summer days, Albion picked a crab apple that was reddening at one side while the monkey scrambled in the tree. He cut it in half and showed Gregory the five-pointed star that they could see, the case with white unripe seeds in it. "Perhaps that had something to do with our idea of shapes and numbers," he said. Then he took a china plate with a raised rim. He found a wine bottle cork and loosely tied the eye of a meat skewer to it. He dug the tines of three forks into the cork and raised it so that it sat on a tripod on the plate. He stuck the crab apple on the bottom of the skewer so that the point swung back and forth just clear of the plate. Then he poured salt at each end of the skewer's swing so that the point cut a groove in it.

"Now watch," he said. He moved the plate around slightly in a sun-wise direction. The skewer point continued to swing but cut new grooves in the salt.

"But why is that? The marks on the salt should be in the same place."

"That's the point," Albion said. "Imagine there was a pane of glass standing where the skewer with the apple weight is swinging. That would be a plane. The skewer is a pendulum. The pendulum keeps swinging on the same plane even though the plate has been turned round. It is like the earth circling around the sun, and the fact that there are different marks when the plate is turned makes it clear to us that the earth itself is turning around as it circles around the sun."

"Is the earth really spinning, Albion?"

"It surely is. That's why the sun comes up in the east every morning."

He got out the Tarot circle and this time did a more complicated foretelling for Charlotte. It showed that while she was still changing, the forces of plenty and satisfaction were still about her. The men and women who entered and left her life did not seem to wish her any ill but as usual it was a question of the way in which she took advantage of all these things.

"You one side other very good again," Mr Cheng said when they went into the restaurant but he seemed to be doubtful about his life. "I have plenty Chinese mushroom tonight but poem not come right way. You help?"

"Of course we will if we can?"

"Writing say, '*wu* and *zhuwu* and *wuzhu*'. I can not say English. It mean person who see picture in wind."

"A kind of witch," Charlotte said.

"A shaman or shamaness — that's what they are called, I think."

"Man who write say '*pin*' — will marry her but many sufferings. She wash her hair. She not eat proper. She look for wise words from strong people. Blood, ash come. Water come. Water come out of jar. She hope." Elegant Cheng walked away from them. A girl began to move between the tables.

"I can't keep up with you," Charlotte said. "First you have Mary. Then you have Jean."

"How do you know about Jean?"

"Oh, Henrietta knows everything that goes on in the town. She told me."

"I just had to make up my mind about things."

"But you are still my friend?"

"Of course I am your friend."

"And you are coming with us?"

"It will be very special for me. Please, Charlotte, do not have any doubt."

Henry came up to Lancaster House with his dray, his long whip cracking over eight bullocks led by Prince on the near side. On the rear they put up a cover with a sofa where Charlotte could dress and sleep. Dan brought a two-horse waggon with two saddle horses tethered behind. They loaded it with hay and firewood for the long Dunstan road. After that there would be public and accommodation houses where they could stay and buy food. They stretched heavy tarpaulins over the hay. Gregory would stay at home to be looked after by the other women.

Far out on the Lammermores where the Dunstan Road curved south of the Rock and Pillar Range, Albion, sitting on some coils of rope, could look back to the east over endless acres of tawny tussock, over the hillocks and gullies where the tussock stood shining in the lowering sun as high as a waggon wheel, as high as a man although it was shorter near the wheel ruts of the road where stock had passed. There was no wind. He could not see any clouds in the sky which was hard in the west. Henry and Dan stood together. Henry, the light shining around his hat, pointed north-west with his whip handle where the Dunstan mountains were black. Dan moved about in clothes outlined with gold, talking. In the emptiness he heard Charlotte's boots clatter on the waggon deck, then on the steps from the driver's seat. Horses and bullocks stood roped and chained to the waggon wheels, eating their hay. The bullocks could have been set to range, to be rounded up in the morning, but Henry, in this unknown country, had thought it better to chain them. Far to the east Albion thought he could see a slight lowering of the ground where the Deep Stream lay and his pond had been. They must be clear, by now, of Dr McIvor's lease.

"It's New Year's Eve — come and see," Charlotte called, waving papers about. "It's New Year's Eve! In a few hours it will be 1870 at last. Do you know that in the town we have left there are more than twenty thousand people! You couldn't believe it out here. And there have been more than five men to one woman at times back there. And there are two and a half thousand Chinese people in Otago. Let's make a fire. But come here, all of you, and I will show you where we are to go." She spread out Logan's map as they came to the waggon, shoving the snorting bullocks away.

They saw that there was a mark at the third gully up the river from Dunstan. There was a frog sign and the number 60N. "Look. We have to go sixty paces up hill from the frog and that's where he got the bath rocks." She put another piece of paper over it. "And here — this is Skippers Canyon, up the Shotover River on the way to Queenstown. We have to climb over this road and then down into the river at its top. There is a U-shaped valley high above the gold diggings. He has marked it with M. We will find the mud there. It will be about a week's journey from here."

"This is very broken country," Dan said. "I picked up a bit of geology in the desert and it looks to me as if these mountains are in folds and what I hear is the inland mountains are made of blocks tilted up so they're all jagged."

They had not known that Henry was musical but he brought out an accordion as they built a fire. "I play to my beasts when I feel lonely on the road," he said, embarassed but apparently determined. He played *Comin' Through the Rye* and *Drink To Me Only* and then *The Lonely Ash Grove*, and had a shot at *Danny Boy* while they piled wood on the fire. Very slow and lugubrious, Henry played *The Star of the County Down*. There were no shadows in the tussock and Albion thought of the schist pillars of the mountains standing above the soil which had been worn away and their lingering shapes in the dusk, spectres like the black shag he had shot so long ago from the top of his scarecrow and, when he thought of it, just as impermanent. He remembered that Barclay had told him there was an old Maori proverb which said that people would die or move away but the land, which would endure for ever, would not change. That was clearly not so as all his reading had proved, and had been proved by the white men who first walked over these hills, men like James Hector on the Acclimatisation Society committee who fifteen years earlier in Scotland had had to take a university degree in medicine because no other science was taught. They were very small as they danced at midnight to Henry's accordion, and sang *Auld Lang Syne*. Charlotte's hand felt damp.

Heat roared at them down the river gorge at Dunstan. They sheltered in one of the many public houses and got feed for the animals there. They continued to Logan's gully, left the waggons picketed there, and walked to look for the frog. It was hard to see at first, among all the other rocks, but Charlotte suddenly called them to look — there was a gleam of dirty white among the tussock which turned out not to be a quartz outcrop. They had not brought a pick but Albion could see that old earth covered a seam of the white rock like the rocks they had put in the bath to make the water soft.

"We'll come back for this," Charlotte said. "We can load up the horse cart with it on the way back." Albion thought, with a sense of wonder, that she was so light about it. She had a total conviction that they would collect her mud and return in good order. When they reached the Molyneaux River below the Pisa Range, still snowy and towering like the Rock and Pillar, they had to find a ford upstream. She had brought soap and made them sit almost naked in the sun while she washed their clothes. Henry, white under his shirt, asked if the sun would hurt him but Dan said it would be good for him as long as he did not have to stay too long undressed in it.

In the distance they could see the faint lines of water races along the hillside where water had been carried to sluices for the cradles of alluvial mining. The miners, Albion was forced to remember, had used only a line, a plumb bob and a set square to measure the correct fall in the race so that water would run along it . . . and all that nearly naked in this sun, or picking away at frozen soil when winter came. Happy in clean clothes they sang as Henry plodded into Cromwell and dry lodgings.

High on the Skippers Pass, south of Coronet Peak, Henry had to unchain the bullocks to manoeuvre the dray around a bend that doubled back on itself. "The trouble with drays is bullocks don't give any braking power," he said. He looked down the long winding hill to the bottom of the gorge. It looked too steep to travel. "You'll have to tie the cart to the dray and let the horses come by themselves and help me pull back on the brake lever. All the way down."

The river rapids crashed up to them. Then, at the bottom, they continued up an incline until a blueish slip of broken stones smothered the track with scree. "It'll shift. I reckon it'll shift under me and bury me if I go across there - waggon and bullocks and all."

"Oh, come on Henry — other men must have made it over," Charlotte said, and when they reached the far side she suddenly shouted, above the river noise, "There it is!" They could see a mining village with a few small poplar trees and a stone-walled school and church. Above it hung the U-shaped valley marked on the map with a silver trickle of water running from it, very steep, almost a precipice but covered with ferns and heaths and small veronica shrubs. "That's where my mud is. Stop the waggon, Henry." The whip fled out and cracked beyond the leaders. It would be cold at night, Albion thought. They were above three thousand feet. He would be glad of his greatcoat. He would get them to roll up under the tarpaulin when they slept under the dray.

She made them strap bags to their backs and coils of line when they climbed up to the valley. It was full of water, stretching back in a U tipped over. It was like a hot-house. A little wind, now warm, drifted down from the peaks above but the walls were covered with daisies and buttercups, blue-bells, sweet-smelling broom and mountain wineberry shrubs with hardly any leaves, creepers with blue berries and starry carpets like cushions. Panting, she waded into the lake outlet, her boots and skirt soaked. She scooped below the water with her hands and brought them up full of dripping green silt. "We've found it!" She bent her head and plastered her face. Water pressed her blouse to her chest. She began to laugh.

"That's all very well but there's not enough of it," Albion called.

"Well, we'll just have to wade into the lake and dig it up," she said.

There was no way to stop her, Albion thought when they came down to the animals. They would have to think of a method.

"Needles," he said. "We have no needles."

"Yes, we have. I brought some, and thread in case the harness broke," Dan said.

"Well, I've been thinking. There's some goats up there. They must have escaped from the miners' camp some time. We could shoot them and blow up the skins. Then we can cut a raft out of the tarpaulin and cut osier poles from the poplars to stretch it out. We could float that with the goat skins and go out into the lake and shovel up the mud onto it."

"And make a pile of it," said Henry. "And the water would drain away and we could bring the mud down."

"It'll work," Dan said. "In the end we had to carry water like that in the desert." That night Charlotte brought out a bottle of brandy and they were warm by their fire. "We have almost conquered the mud," she said, and poured more into their pannikins before she went to her sofa.

Albion thought of the water races and how slow that had been. There were more flowers in the valley than he had ever seen. They would have to get used to slowness and work carefully and aim straight at the goats, remembering that on steep places the range of shot was shortened by elevation if they had to shoot up or down.

Floating out the pontoon, he felt proud. It had not been hard to make and it held together while they shovelled mud up from the shallow bottom where it had fallen as the lake froze each year. Then they filled the bags and carefully lowered them, tied to the line, down the slope to Skippers.

They found that it was early in February when the waggon was laden with its ton and a half and they could leave.

Charlotte said she was praying no rain would fall before they reached the rocks in Logan's gully. Albion said that it would not matter if it did rain because the rocks had experienced the weather for millions of years, hadn"t they? As it was they filled the bags quickly, picking deep into the seam. Dan even contrived to blow up part of the entrance with gunpowder which he packed in their teapot with a fuse of plaited tussock stems in the spout, which made it quicker to take the load but it took them twice as long to amble into Dunedin.

"Magnesium sulphate," said John Wilkes wisely, looking at the rocks. "It is what Epsom salts are made of. I know because I've tasted them. It is made when almost all the water is taken out of the chemicals in sea water — by evaporating it and by squeezing. All in a certain proportion, of course."

"But that's why it works. That's why it's good for arms and legs in the bath. Holy smoke — I will write to Mr Lancaster straight away."

SAN FRANCISCO
MARCH 29, 1870

Dear Charlotte,
Thank you for your commodious letter with all its news of your many endeavours. I have studied it carefully and decided to take certain steps.

You seem to have come across some natural resources of Otago from which much good might come. I am impressed with your ideas and would like to offer advice in the hope that you may greatly benefit from your enterprise.

First of all I think that you should look to proper packaging if you are to sell the material you have discovered. When I left Dunedin a glass works was being started at Archerfield and I suggest that you have them make you jars. I think that blue would be appropriate for the mud you have obtained and that your bath salts might adequately be contained in a green jar. You should have the Otago

Daily Times and Witness Company *print you some handsome labels that may be pasted on. I suggest that you call the spirogyra mud 'Charlotte's Gold Cream' and the salts 'Charlotte's Bath Pamper' or something like that. I know that you have obtained flower oils from Gregory's father but I am sending you a flask of bergamot oil which I think would be useful for the facial preparation. It is made from the skin of Seville oranges which are beginning to grow well in California and would make a very fresh and clean scent. You could add flower oils to the salts as you consider fit.*

I have thought about the problem of your rocks. A kind of stamper has been invented here for crushing quartz rocks to get at the gold through the mercury amalgamation process and I think that a small battery of this kind would be adequate to reduce your rocks to a powder. Accordingly I have arranged to have the battery sent to you on the S.S. Waitahuna *which will be sailing from here to Port Chalmers on the service next month. You will need to acquire a small steam engine to turn the battery wheels but I imagine that you will be easily able to do that.*

As I have said, I am very willing to arrange for the sale of your products here and in Sydney but I cannot advise you too strongly that you must form a company. I am willing to be a silent partner with you as Chairman and under you such persons as you appoint. It is essential that you have a good accountant for the company books and my agent in Dunedin will advise you on how to set the company up.

I have always had faith in you, dear Charlotte, and now everything that I have felt for you is being justified. With every loving wish . . .

Albion made up his mind to invest his last thousand pounds in the company which Charlotte decided to call Pampering Activities Limited — "PAL," she said. "Isn't that a good name —

and I will be safe with you as a director and I will ask Thora to become the accountant because she knows how to run a business."

She had an open shed built in the garden for the sacks of bounty they had gathered, and sent Henry off again with three trusted men to dig more mud and rocks.

At night Albion could lie awake listening to the ocean rollers break from the south onto St Clair beach, pounding over barren White Island that stood alone off shore.

"Mr Lancaster — he is being very kind to us but I don't even know what he looks like."

"Oh, he was quite clean shaven as I remember him but he had a moustache, a rather bristly one that I didn't like. It scraped and tickled me. And he kept very good fingernails — you know some men would have hands that were all hard and cracked but his fingernails were shiny. He would cut them so they were just white at the ends. He would even polish them. And he was very tall with blue eyes and a gold watch chain across his tummy. His tummy was very flat. His hair was turning grey and he always slept with his window wide open so the air was cold and fresh, he said, but it pained in my nose. And he walked. He strode everywhere — down the Peninsula, over Flagstaff and Mt Cargill. He always drank coffee. He said he'd had far too much tea."

"But he never made demands on you?"

"He was so generous. I did everything that I could for him."

The stamper arrived, built up and very heavy with its trough for the stone and its hammers that would clatter up and down. With Henry still up country Dan had to hire another bullock waggon. "It's like old times!" he shouted as he cracked his whip up McLaggan street. He rigged ropes and pullies and slid the stamper on rollers into the open shed, and John said that he had found a steam engine just the right size to turn the wheels. Dan went to Brighton for a load of coal. John coupled the engine drive to the stamper wheels and Albion oiled it and fired the boiler. Charlotte loaded the trough and put a bucket under the end for the ground salts. The monkey hid from the noise.

She took Albion to the printers, she took him to the glass works, she had him make up wooden crates and get straw to pack the jars which she had him label. 'Charlotte's Gold Cream' was carefully mixed with bergamot oil and ladled into the pots. 'Charlotte's Bath Pamper' was measured out. 'Put one tablespoon in the bath.' Thora and Yvonne had decided that that was the right amount to make the soap bubbly. They had put the cream on their faces too and declared it very refreshing. In a fit of curiosity Albion smeared some on his own face but did not enjoy the stiffness of it when it was dry because his looks were no longer mobile.

By the end of the year money was beginning to come to them through the bank. Thora was very proud. She gave up her sewing factory and Charlotte appointed Yvonne sales manager. She asked Henrietta to open a shop on Princes Street and Albion invited the Lebanese tinker where he had lodged to place his wares there, too. It was New Years' Day, 1871, and he said, "It is very strange. I did not think that I would ever become a man of commerce." His money was making a return. Steam blew around the engine, and the hammers of the stamper rattled even though it was a holiday. All Cheng could say, when they went for supper, was to remind them that wars were won by winning the battle and not in the fighting.

"If I had a suit cut and made for myself and bought a top hat I would still be fighting," he said to Charlotte while the violin played eerily, and girls, who seemed much younger now, began to move about the tables. "I will instead buy some new underwear, a shirt or two and some more of the same clothes."

"But we will soon have plenty, Albion."

"I think I shall dress the way I have always dressed." He began to plan a boat house. He knew that the Brighton River was wide and long enough for boats to be rowed on it. He could have the timber sawn and a house built there, and boats made and they would be used by rich people who would go there from Dunedin to have a holiday. It was only a few hours away in a good coach. The roof of the house would have a shallow slope and the boats could be pulled up or moored to a jetty under a verandah. You would be able to hire a boat and lie back on the stream while sea birds flew overhead and ducks quacked about and herons hissed and you could still hear waves breaking on the rock-bound bay with its white sand that faced north-east. It would soon get about that there was a holiday cove there, and pleasure to be had. "It's a dream I have," he said when he told her. "Picture a lean white boat with a filligreed iron seat in the back where you would recline in a straw sun bonnet while you watched me row."

"You're just a romantic, Albion. That's too ideal for words."

"But it will come. Wait and see . . . Meanwhile, do you mind writing to Mr Lancaster for me and asking him to send a fishing rod — one made of greenheart which is a tree found in Panama or thereabouts. They use it for rods to fish for rainbow trout in California."

"You're a director. Why don't you write to him yourself?"

"Listen to that violin. Isn't it extraordinary that for far more than a thousand years the Church thought that the only music fit to be heard in a temple was the sound of a human voice — in spite of the fact that the Bible records many musical instruments like harps and psalters and drums and cymbals and 'sounding brass'. Yes. I will write to him."

TEN

Gregory was twelve. Albion had recouped his investment many times and Thora was wearing severe black dresses cut in the finest material while Yvonne chose bright browns and yellows although contriving a severe look. John Wilkes had rigged a long pipe with a whistle onto the boiler. When it sounded the women Charlotte employed to clean and pack the mud and salts would come out or go into the shed in the cow paddock with sunlight on their faces as if they felt at peace to be there. They were as if they were in water even though the north-east wind often blew, and when winter came the sun would go early behind the Mornington hill and the place would grow damp. John warned that it could not be long before the mining inspectors began to question their supplies, even though they were not gold.

"It is late January," Albion said. "If any of my fish are still alive they will be grown in the sea by now. They will be coming back up the river to the Deep Stream to lay their eggs."

"How hot it is . . . Perhaps you could catch a fish."

"We could stay at the accommodation house at Hindon. We could take the carriage out from there and walk down into the gorge. It would be rough but not too far. Will you come with me?"

In the low sun he thought of how he had become thirty-six and was still trying to move slowly. Dan had fetched two horses and harnessed them to the brougham. A cold southerly wind had passed over and the sky would be clear for a few days. While he waited for Charlotte he watched the horses hanging still in the stable yard. The monkey had come and was clambering in the spokes of the carriage wheels, gambolling like a sprite, some other kind of creature that belonged in the trees, among the fruits at the edge of the garden beyond the washing wire. As he jumped down in front of the wheel the near side horse kicked back with its hoof. Tiny was thrown back against the wheel and lay like a lump of brown wool. Albion stepped forward and picked him up. The monkey lay in his arms. His hands could feel the crushed chest. It made no sound and then slowly turned its square and somehow smoothed face towards the sun. It opened its eyes towards the brightness and stretched out its right hand, pointing for a moment. Then it gripped Albion's fingers very tightly. It held and pulled as if asking him to go with it. It pressed into his shoulder as if it were a pillow. Its eyes crinkled and it vomited down him, a quartzy fluid with lumps of old fruit that seemed to have no smell. Then it sank in him and was dead.

He realised that Charlotte, in a white blouse with red embroidery at the throat that seemed too gay, was standing by him. He wanted to ask her to cover her head with a black shawl but no words came to him.

She was quite crisp. He dug a hole in the garden while she found a bed sheet to wrap the body. Mavis went to the creek and came back with a piece of drift wood almost in the shape of a cross. Dolly brought a bottle of wine from the cellar and put it out on the kitchen table. She made tea and put a fruit cake on a plate. Nobody spoke. He thought he saw a face in the beech tree from the corner of his eye and did not want to look.

"Do you still want to go?" Dan asked softly when the earth had been turned.

"Oh yes. When we have had something to refresh ourselves. The girls will have to tell Gregory when he gets home."

He went to put on a clean shirt. He supposed that he ought to be flattered that she still wanted to leave. Nobody had cried and that was what he felt like. Suddenly there had been a 'not life' and he struggled to understand it and to comfort himself with things that he had thought before. He could see no sense in this.

"He was a good little monkey," Charlotte said as they drove away, her tears making zig-zags down her cheeks with the rocking of the carriage. "He loved me straight away when Grigori gave him to me. He really looked after us when Gregory was born. He was like a . . . like a . . . a kind of fatherly little monkey, I suppose. That's it. He was like a father to us even though he was so small." He thought that he ought to hold her hand.

Alone on the flat-topped tussock hills the accommodation house could hardly be seen with its mud-brick walls and thatched roof but when they came closer they could see that there was a meat safe in the shade of a group of young pine trees and some apples with lichen already on the branches, and a stunted plum hedge around some potatoes, turnips and parsnips. Inside, the house had rough manuka joists and beams and lacked a ceiling.

"There's not much of a fire place but I get peat from a swamp down in the gully and dry it out," the woman with grey hair and wire-rimmed spectacles said. "And I can cook all right on it. We was very busy when the miners were looking in the river and the shepherds come by often enough and sometimes they bring wild pigs. And I make the plum wine in the autumn — that's always good. I have to cart water in. How long will you be staying?"

"Just two nights, I think."

"Well, the driver can sleep in the bunk room and you two, well there's a bed in another room."

"But we're not . . ."

"Don't worry about that. I knows why youse come out here. They all do. The sheep's been here since 1851 and the house in 1853 and they talk of a railway line up the river but that'll be a long time."

She served them a mutton and apple stew topped with Yorkshire pudding made in her camp oven, and potatoes. "I've got no greens out here. They get burned up in the wind." They drank bitter plum wine.

The bed in the bunk room where he went with Dan in spite of her encouragement was hard and narrow. He thought Dan must have gone to sleep quickly but lay awake, too hot even to doze. Mice and insects scratched in the thatch. He was sure that a mouse fell on him and flung away his blanket in a dark panic at it, trying to calm himself by thinking of himself as a similar creature in the shelter. As he tried not to move in the heat he saw Charlotte, in her long cotton nightdress, come in, drifting, he thought. He felt her hand on his shoulder.

"Come and talk to me," she whispered. "It's so lonely in there and there's all sorts of noises."

Her bed had a hard mattress over a wire mesh that sagged so much a pole had been put up the middle. "It's like bundling, isn't it, with that between us. None the less, I once swore that I would never lie on a bed with a man again."

"It's too hot. But at least the linen is dry. I'd hate to be here in winter. You would hear the wind."

"You can hear it sighing away there now."

"In his play, *The Tempest*, Shakespeare has his monster Caliban say, *Be not afeard. The isle is full of noise, Sounds and sweet airs that give delight and hurt not.* I think he was talking about the world, not just the 'isle'.

"Oh, Albion, I'm so unhappy about the little monkey."

"They say that one door shuts and another door opens."

"Do you think that Tiny would have a hereafter?"

"I don't know about that. I depends on how much you loved him, I suppose."

"You can hold my hand."

"Don't cry any more, Charlotte. We all go to the same thing in the end, don't we."

"That helps. My hand feels sweaty."

He counted the rafters, seeing the figures one two three four, like domino spots in Marching time, feeling the bark. "When my father died he held my hand. He was sick on it. Then my mother didn't last much longer."

"You were all alone then. How did you cope?"

"Just like you and the monkey, I suppose. I cried once — when my father was in the coffin. In the church."

"I don't want to cry. Stop me crying, Albion. You can, you know."

"I don't think that I know much at all. Unfortunately there is a difference between what I believe and what I think — between knowledge and the truth."

"Those words seem all the same to me." She held his hand and shook her head on the pillow.

"Well, if you were a nun in Naples," he said sleepily, "you could join a holy procession with a bottle of milk that you would swear was mother's milk eighteen hundred and seventy years old that you would swear came from a carved statue of Mary the Madonna. You would swear and swear that it had turned liquid on the day. That's belief, I think. It's neither knowledge nor the truth. But it's just terribly hot. Go to sleep now. I'll go back when you go to sleep."

He went to the bunk room in the early morning, still feeling the touch of her hand and hearing the deep breathing that came to her suddenly. His bones and his body still seemed to be heaving with the brougham and the horses' feet were loud. He tried to think of sun shining in fur and became more cool. The beginning of life was like the way changes happened in a kaleidoscope, he thought — every shift in the crystals made a different picture ordered by the mirrors. The origin of life must lie in an uncountable number of shifts, making an uncountable number of pictures organised by light passing over an uncountable number of mirrors. Life that reproduced itself was but one of an uncountable number of possible responses to an uncountable number of mirrored possibilities.

Dan woke him in the dawn. He said they would have a long day if he wanted to fish. He took them out along a track to the end of a ridge above the river gorge where there seemed to be a sheep track down.

"I'll come back in the afternoon."

"But we might be late. It'll just about be dark."

He knew that Charlotte would be nimble going down the track in her denim skirt. He carried his greenheart rod carefully and felt the weight of his rucksack with his gear, with bread and meat. His legs seemed to shake as he swung down behind her. The cold smell of the river came up faintly and he thought that the smoky pollen of lupins was mingled warmly with it. A few English foxgloves stood tall on the track already, like pink and white pagodas set in their fleshy pale leaves. The blue lion, he remembered, was looking to the right, with its right foot on a cub. It must have been a puppy because it was not a lion but a dog. The river seemed to be barking at them from among the boulders. Now he could see the bottom of the stream pool where it fed the river, and saw Charlotte there, under water for a moment, her thighs spreading while his whole being rushed out to her. Linger a while, he thought. Stay there under the water and I will sweep over you. His elation became mixed with the fine pull of the line on the rod in his hands and his hope that a live fish would come to it. Then they waded across the downstream shallows to the fan he had camped on when he discovered the outlet.

"You will get too much sun if you watch me fishing."

"I like it here. I'll be all right."

"No. I'll make some shade for you first."

He went into a stand of manuka scrub and cut some poles, the wood staining red at the cut, for the four corners of a shelter, a bower for her, he thought, while the manuka dust tickled in his nose. He propped the poles in piles of stones with crosspieces for roof beams. He went up to the beginning of the bush and cut tree fern fronds to lace into a roof. Centipedes and wetas fell in his hair. Dark spider orchids bloomed in the moss at his feet and some bright lantern berry. Then he cut more fern and spread it on the stones in a bed.

"You'll be comfortable there," he said. "And I can build a fire in front of it when the day gets on."

His hands shook slightly as he took out his box of casts. They were coiled there, damp enough in cotton waste to keep the gut strong, and he bent one onto the linen line of his reel. Then he sought a feather fly, choosing a long Dorothy pattern with a yellow chenille body bound with silver wire, red hackles at the tail and throat and banded black and white feathers along the top of the hook. Who was Dorothy?

He forgot Charlotte. Where the shingle fan met the river he stripped line from his reel and cast, up stream and across, not far enough, he thought, as the current carried fly and line in an arc downstream. He held the line, stripped more from the reel, retrieved and cast again into the rapids where they flattened out. After half an hour he was prepared to give up. He looked up at the sky above the gorge and saw a harrier circling. Some terns hawked by close to the water. Above the noise he heard the heavy flap of a black shag going upstream.

He cast again. The fly was hit. He lifted the rod tip to set the hook. The fish ran and he braked the reel, afraid of losing his line. He turned the fish just above the lower rapids and began to play it fiercely, reeling in and letting out but keeping a firm pressure all the time. Not all that heavy, he thought of the fish, but it was active and he worked it closer by walking up the fan and retrieving as he walked forward again. He saw it then, silver and rose, turning on its side as he brought it towards the bank. Slowly he eased it in and then, in the shallows, he bent and caught it by the wrist, the column of the body just before the tail, and hauled it ashore. He was shaking. He held the wrist and bashed the salmon's head with the stone. It stiffened and died.

When he slid his knife in the vent and opened the gut he was frightened and amazed at its fullness of eggs — hundreds of orange-red spheres that he had to lift from her by the handful and throw out into the stream, more than a thousand eggs floating away from his dripping hand. He cleaned out the cavity and cleanly cut away the gills. His stomach knotted against his belt and his upper arms quivered.

"First fruits," he said to Charlotte as he stood up with his fingers in the throat. Watching, she had come to stand beside him. "I'll have to dry it. I'll have to send it to the British Museum in London so that they can identify it properly as an Atlantic salmon, the very first to be caught here. It'll take months but I'll have to do it. I'm sure it's a salmon. I think there's the right number of bones in the anal fin. That's how you tell, or one way. Oh Charlotte — they're coming back, the salmon I let go. It's all right. I did the right thing." He began to walk with his rod, swinging the fish, and she followed him.

Lying in the bower on the fern fronds he thought that it was not so much the feeling in his thighs, although that was like nettle rash both stinging and itching, but the colours of blood that seemed to rush to his head, red at first, blazing red tinged with gold and then blue and then purple, beating in his head so that he saw it even though he opened his eyes wide and saw her face under him and her hair spread out on the green fern and felt her pressing up to meet him, and her nipples hard against him and her mouth together with his as if there were only one and the ringing in his ears to which he could give no heed because of the sound they made together.

He counted empty mussel shells to slow himself. A golden rain sprang from the rapids and the lupins and the foxgloves, the bullrushes and the thatch, tussock and sky on a sward covered in heart's-ease, and red eggs tumbled slippery down and down in his fingers.

"The British Museum," she said, after a long time. "I swore I would never do that with anyone again but it is so different. I never felt that before. I never did, I promise."

"The Chief Ichthyologist — that's what he's called, I think. Do you really promise? I never felt like that, either."

She laughed when he pulled on his boots and walked naked, wearing just them, with the billy to fill it for tea and, naked, built the fire with driftwood that scratched his thighs.

"I'm hungry," she said when the logs burned down. "Please don't get dressed. I love you like that. I'm quite warm enough, too. I couldn't bear to eat that bread and mutton."

He took up the fish then, and wrapped it tightly in fern leaves. He pushed up the wood and put the fish on the fire. In half an hour he brought it into the bower. They lifted pieces of pink flesh to their mouths and licked. They swallowed and smiled at each other while the juice ran over their bodies.

He caught a piece of flesh on his thumb and flicked it at her with his forefinger. She looked down at it on her breast while he licked it off. They began to lick each other. They licked the fish bones clean after they had eaten all the flesh, and rubbed each other with fern until they were rosy. Albion leaned out and picked up a round stone. He flicked it onto the stream pool and it skipped three times before it sank. "I can even do that sitting down," he said.

"You can do anything," she said, and he felt good because he thought she sounded proud. All without thinking he picked up a piece of fish skin. Oil glistened on the brown arrow marks of flesh grown to it like paint. While she lay back he took up the skin and began to massage her belly with it, round and round. She moved against him as he pressed it and drew him to her. She rocked down with her buttocks and scrunched her toes as he floated on her, as if her body were covered in the same skin as his fingers. He felt, at last he felt, as if he were experiencing all that was most human in himself. He felt her pressing him between her thighs as if she contracted down, inside, about him in her hollows. She became firm in ridges that he felt in radiations with all his heart as he pulled his hips back — one final time before they let go.

"Do you think they could tell anything from a skeleton?" he

asked when he knelt up beside her.

"Bones to fire," she said, and threw the skeleton into the embers.

"Now what'll I do? We ate it instead. We fed on it. Like wasps."

"You know perfectly well that you caught a salmon. You can report it, and they can never take that away from you. Ever."

"Is that the way it always happens? Is that the way it *has* always happened?"

"I don't know and I don't care. It was all . . . it *is* all . . . just what I imagine," she said. And her voice was in song notes, like a bird's.